THE STREETS STAINED MY SOUL

Marcellus Allen

Lock Down Publications and Ca$h
Presents
The Streets Stained My Soul
A Novel by *Marcellus Allen*

Lock Down Publications
P.O. Box 870494
Mesquite, Tx 75187

Copyright 2019 Marcellus Allen
The Streets Stained My Soul

First Edition January 2020
Printed in the United States of America

Lock Down Publications
Like our page on Facebook: Lock Down Publications @
www.facebook.com/lockdownpublications.ldp
Cover design and layout by: **Dynasty Cover Me**
Book interior design by: **Shawn Walker**
Edited by: **Sunny Giovanni**

Stay Connected with Us!

Text **LOCKDOWN** to 22828 to stay up-to-date with new releases, sneak peaks, contests and more…

Thank you!

Submission Guideline.

Submit the first three chapters of your completed manuscript to ldpsubmissions@gmail.com, subject line: Your book's title. The manuscript must be in a .doc file and sent as an attachment. Document should be in Times New Roman, double spaced and in size 12 font. Also, provide your synopsis and full contact information. If sending multiple submissions, they must each be in a separate email.

Have a story but no way to send it electronically? You can still submit to LDP/Ca$h Presents. Send in the first three chapters, written or typed, of your completed manuscript to:

LDP: Submissions Dept
P.O. Box 870494
Mesquite, Tx 75187

DO NOT send original manuscript. Must be a duplicate.

Provide your synopsis and a cover letter containing your full contact information.

Thanks for considering LDP and Ca$h Presents

Marcellus Allen

Chapter 1
Juice

Me and Gunna sat inside the blacked-out Escalade with nothing but money on our minds. But money wasn't given out in the streets; it was taken. Take it or get yours taken; that's the law for the ones that live lawless. So, I felt no compassion or empathy for what was about to be done. *Kill or be killed, eat or be eaten,* I reminded myself as I tucked my chain under the black hoody I had on. The same chain that my big brother Juice had given me right before a bitch nigga took his soul off the earth.

I gritted my teeth at the anger that shot through my body. The pictures ran through my mind. I saw my idol with his face slumped over his steering wheel, dead to this world. His lifeless eyes stared right through mine. I squinted my eyes a few times to block out the images and get back to the task at hand.

I turned down Finesse2Tymes's newest album *Federal 4 Real* down and vented my frustration. "Yo, where the fuck this punk ass Mexican at?" I growled at Gunna. We'd been sitting there for over an hour and I was getting madder by the minute.

"He gon' be here, Blood." He turned to face me. I could see it in his eyes, the thrill of the hunt. He was ready to eat. "He gotta come home. His bitch ain't going for that, trust me." An evil smirk appeared on his face.

I nodded in agreement. Gunna knew exactly what he was talking about since it was his plug that we were waiting on.

"Speakin' of the devil." Gunna nodded at the car that had just pulled into the lot. It definitely was the devil's work that we were on and it wasn't an angel on this earth that could stop the evil we were about to bring.

"About time." I popped the clip out, double checking the bullets, then popped it back in. I slid the ski mask over my face all the while never taking my eyes off the Ford Focus. I looked over at Gunna. He had his mask on now, ready to hunt. I stared at his dreads that were hanging out and remembered from one of those CSI shows how a single strand could get a nigga booked. I touched my neck and felt multiple of my dreads hanging there. *Fuck it,* I thought. Wasn't no point in saying nothing to Gunna 'cause wasn't shit we could do to fix it and I didn't want to jinx it.

"Let's move." Gunna spoke, then crept out like a thief in the night.

I bounced out into the cold night, hand gripping the steel with my heart matching the weather. We waited until the short Mexican walked past us then followed right behind him. There wasn't a soul in the lot or sitting on the steps which wasn't the norm in the Columbia Stations. It usually were a few niggas hanging out all night but with the whole town in a civil war I guess niggas was trying to live. We followed him all the way to his steps before he finally turned around.

All he saw were two masked niggas with heaters aimed right at his face. His hands shot straight up in the air. "What the fuck is this?" He yelled in a thick Spanish accent.

"Say another word, bitch, and they gon' have to ship yo body back to Mexico in a box." I growled. I put the barrel on his forehead, daring him to play with me. He submitted with his words, but I could see the fire in his eyes. I knew at that moment he had to die. There was no way around that. "Now open the door real slow, then walk in with yo hands up. And if you try any heroic shit, I'm gon' kill you and yo bitch." I spat.

Fear and surprise flashed across his eyes before he did what I demanded. He knew we did our homework on his ass. We walked into the semi dark living room then pushed the Mexican down on the couch. I stood over him with the banger ready to go off at the slightest act of aggression. While Gunna went and closed the door, I started the interrogation.

"Look, Felipè, we know your wife Christina is back there sleeping, and you don't want us to wake her up, trust me. We want the money and the dope, and we want all of it right now."

Gunna started patting him down, making sure he ain't have a pistol on him. He pulled a switchblade from his jacket pocket. Once Gunna finished I continued my speech.

"And I don't wanna hear that *it's at another spot* shit either.

Whatever you got over there you can keep but we want everything you got in this spot." I demanded.

He sat there staring into my eyes, trying to place them or burn them in his memory for a later date. I wasn't worried about either one though. He didn't know me, and I had no intentions of letting him live to see another day. A wide smirk spread across his face. "Listen. Amigo, you don't wanna do this. I work for very important people that won't appreciate you taking their property. Why don't you and your silent friend here just leave while you can? It's not too late, Amigo." He said the shit with a straight face.

Gunna slapped him across the face with the pistol. He fell to the floor moaning with blood pouring down his face. I exhaled my frustration. I knew where he was headed and hoped to avoid it. Gunna told me that the Mexican considered himself a tough guy. But even tough guys had weaknesses.

"Aight, I tried to warn you. Now I'ma show you what that Cartel talking will get you." I spat.

Gunna forced him up then led us down the hallway to his bedroom. I opened the door to my left just to make sure nobody was hiding in there. It looked like his office so we kept on going.

"Make one sound and I'ma crush yo bitch right in front of you. We could've did this shit the easy way but you just had to be hard." I growled in his ear when we pulled up to the final door.

I stared at the blood dripping down his face then glanced in his eyes once more. He still had defiance in them, but I could see his soul cracking. His weakness was just the same as any other man's. His wife. And we were only a few feet away from exploiting it.

Gunna stepped into the room first, ready to kill whatever moved the wrong way, but nothing moved. A Mexican bitch laid on her stomach wearing only her bra and panties, knocked the fuck out. He gave Felipè a thumbs up then placed the barrel on top of her temple.

"Don't fuckin' touch her." Felipè growled like that shit was supposed to scare us.

Gunna ignored his dry threat and started pressing the heat into her head harder and harder until she finally opened her eyes. The fear was evident instantly. She woke up to her worse nightmare, but that was her problem, not ours.

"Papi, what's going on?" She tried to choke back her tears but they still slid out.

"Everything's gonna be fine, baby." Felipè falsely assured her.

I crashed the heat down on the top of his skull, dropping his tough guy ass to the floor. *Fuck wrong with this nigga?* "Shut yo bitch ass up, nigga, you ain't runnin' shit!" I stood over him yelling right in his face. "And, bitch, stop cryin' before we pop yo top just for the fuck of it." She did her best to muffle her crying but all that sniffling and shit was pissing me off too. I felt like we had been in there far too long and needed to speed the process up dramatically. I focused back on Felipè. "Here's the triv, Felipè. You gon' take us to the work right now or we gon' crush y'all and head home. Now tell me how you wanna do this, 'cause yo bitch don't look ready to die."

He looked up at me and knew that I wasn't playing no more games. "Alright, I'll take you to it. Just take the gun off of her head, Amigo."

"Naw, the gun gon' stay right where it's at, Amigo, in case you try any lone desperado shit. Now get up and take me to the money."

He got up all wobbly and holding the new knot that was exploding from his head. "It's down the hall in the other room." He gave in.

"I'ma go get this bag. You already know what to do if shit ain't right," I spoke, then led Felipè down the hall.

My heart sped up with each step we took toward the room. I needed that bag bad as a muthafucka, quiet as it was kept. Nobody could tell due to my appearance and jewelry, but I was damn near broke. Shit had been bad ever since O-Dawg and them Mob niggas fell off the throne. But I was determined to claw my way back up to the top by any means.

"Where's it at?" were my worlds as soon as we stepped inside.

"In the safe under the desk."

I looked over his shoulder and saw the safe sitting right in the middle. "A'ight, nigga, open it up real slow and don't try none of that Steven Seagal shit either. Open it, then lay face down on the floor. Anything other than that gon' get you and yo bitch killed real quick."

"I know. I'm not gon' try anything."

I nodded at the safe and followed him over to it. Soon as his knees touched the floor, I pressed the barrel to the back of his head. He opened it under my close scrutiny then put his face in the carpet. I started placing stacks and stacks of money on the floor. My quick estimate put the bread around a hundred thousand. I realized I didn't have nothing to put the money in and started looking around for something to use. I couldn't find a bag, pillowcase or nothing. *Fuck!*

"Nigga, where the fuck a bag at? And where all the dope at?" I demanded.

I looked around again and still couldn't find nothing to use. I stared at the pile of money and really didn't want to leave it, not even for a second. As bad as my luck had been in the last year, I wouldn't have been surprised if the shit disappeared as soon as I walked out. *Fuck it.* I had to go get the dope anyways out of the kitchen.

I forced Felipè up and out of the room. I turned around in the hallway just to make sure the money hadn't disappeared. "Which cabinet the dope in?" I demanded after we made it to the kitchen.

"The drugs are above the stove and the bags are in the drawer right there." He pointed out the two spots.

"Grab the dope and set it on the counter piece by piece. Any funny shit and I'ma spray yo brains all across the stove." I felt he needed to be reminded that I wasn't to be fucked with.

"I know, Amigo."

I watched him slowly reach over the stove, open the cabinet and pull out a brick of cocaine. He held it up for me to see then set it down. He repeated the process with another brick, and I felt so much joy rush through my heart. But when he pulled out a pound of meth, that's when I really got excited. "What the fuck is that?"

"Crystal Meth, Amigo." He said like I really didn't know.

I just wasn't expecting it 'cause Gunna only described him as a coke dealer. I'd only seen meth once or twice in my life and didn't know shit about selling it. But I did know there was no way in the world I was leaving it. Hungry niggas scraped their plates, not leaving a crumb. I was hungry. "I know what it is, nigga. How many more are left?"

"There's four more pounds in here."

"Keep stacking them then, nigga, and hurry up." I opened a drawer that the bags were in. I wanted to speed the process up.

"I know that's Gunna in there with my wife." Felipè's words sent chills through my veins as I searched for the bags.

Something felt wrong deep in my gut. There was no fear in his voice any longer. I spun around like my life depended on it.

Boom! Boom! Boom! Boca! Boca! Boca! Boca!

He was just getting ready to put a slug in me as I spun, then dropped to the floor. All of my bullets found new homes in his chest as I fired from the floor. His pistol flew across the kitchen as he slid to the ground with both hands glued to his chest. He was gasping for air while blood poured from his mouth and his wounds.

"Stupid muthafucka," I spat while picking myself up. "Now look at yo dumb ass; bleeding to death all over yo own kitchen."

"Fuck you." He spat a blob of blood on the floor.

"What the fuck happened?" Gunna entered the kitchen by himself.

"Nigga, where the bitch at?" I didn't hear no gunshot and didn't need her calling the police.

"I knocked her out; we good. Damn, Blood, why you pop 'em?" He asked. I could hear him smiling behind the mask.

"The nigga tried to pull a trick play on me." I pointed at Felipè's gun on the floor.

"Is that right?" He spoke in a menacing voice as he walked up on Felipè. Gunna hated when somebody fucked with me more than when somebody fucked with him. So, I already knew where this was headed.

"Yeah, and his bitch ass said yo name before he tried to end me." I added fuel to the fire.

Gunna's mask was off in a split second. He smiled at his prey. "Here's Johnny!" He did his best Jack Nicholson impersonation while he aimed his heat right at his face. "You should've fronted me the work and none of this would've happened."

"Fuck you, puta. Fuckin' nigger." Felipè spat with all the courage he could muster.

"I want you to picture this big ass nigger dick going in and out of yo wife's mouth before I pop her top, bitch."

Boom! Boom! Boom! Boom!

Half his face was blown off as he collapsed on his back. I stared down at his lifeless body not having a drop of sympathy for him. He knew what he signed up for when he entered this shit.

"I told you he was a ill nigga."

"Yeah, his ill ass almost offed me too." I was still mad as a muthafucka at myself.

"Next time keep yo eyes on the victim and not the prize, then you won't almost get killed."

I handed him some trash bags. "Here. Bag the work up while I go get the money. Let's hurry up before the bitch wakes up and we gotta crush her." I stopped by the bedroom to make sure she wasn't up trying to call the police or some shit.

Damn. She was slumped on the floor, laying on her stomach with blood leaking from her head. *This nigga might've killed her,* I told myself, then jetted to the money. A rush of relief hit me when my eyes found the stacks of money. I dropped to my knees and started throwing them dead presidents into the bag like my life depended on it. Shit, to me it did. When I turned around Gunna was standing in the doorway with his heat out and crazed look in his eyes. We'd been crime partners since grade school so I knew exactly what he was thinking.

"Not gon' happen., that's gon' make us ten times hotter. C'mon it's time to shake." I stared him up and down then left without another word. *Crazy ass nigga.*

***

It took a lil' over two hours to count up all the money and weigh the dope. But not one complaint fell out of either one of our mouths. We exchanged our goon faces for one another with deep smiles on them. We were smiling from ear to ear like we had just won the lottery instead of took a soul off this earth for the love of the almighty dollar.

"A'ight, that's sixty-five thousand a piece, a brick and two pounds of meth for me." I told Gunna while I stood up to stretch. I let him keep the extra pound of meth without a second thought. It was his lash in the first place, and even if it wasn't I still wouldn't have given a fuck. That's how it was between us. We just wanted to see each other shine.

"And I'ma holla at my mans to see what the ticket is for the meth. You want me to dump yours off too or what?" He asked.

"Yeah, you can take them muthafuckaz for me. I don't know what they go for, but I know them Mexicans and white boys be getting rich off that shit. And right now, I needa get rich 'cause being close to the bottom ain't what it is. Shit been fucked up since all those snitch niggas took O-Dawg off the streets. Bitch ass niggas." It made my soul burn just thinking about how dirty my nigga got done.

"The snitches been winning out here like a muthafucka, Blood. We needa start shootin' them bitch niggas in the head every time we see one. On me!"

I loved my city to death, but we were suffering from the same rat curse that every urban section in America was suffering from. All the so called real niggas were either turning snitch or embracing snitches like they were real niggas. And when a real nigga spoke the truth about it, everybody turned their backs on them like they were in the wrong. Like they were the ones that was doing the snitching. But the coldest thing about the whole epidemic was that most of the rats were cold killaz. It was nothing to hear about some snitch nigga splittin' somebodies top, especially for calling them a snitch, which they were.

"You ain't never lied." I shook my head while envisioning cutting out the tongue of a snitch bitch. The only thing I hated more than snitches was the nigga who killed my big brother. "I know you ain't forgot how I did that pussy half-dead for snitching on O-Dawg." I smirked at the memory.

"Yeah, you a ill nigga for that, but you shoulda came to the Gunna. I coulda shown you how to do it much better." He said mocking A-Wax from Menace to Society.

We busted out laughing. Something told me I needed to holla at O-Dawg and extend my love. I hadn't heard from my nigga since the day he got sentenced, and that was over eight months ago. *I gotta write 'em.*

"Yo, why I keep hearing that them Goonie niggas want yo body in a casket, Blood? We needa stop playin' and go suit up on them pussies. TJ, Omar, Flash and Mask feel the same way too." Gunna changed topics. I found it funny how fast his facial expression switched from happiness to homicidal in a split second. But that's how my nigga lived his life. From one extreme to the next.

"I'm not worried about them suckaz. If they really felt some type of way about Lil' Shawn, then they would've been got at me. Them niggas just fishing for information. They don't know shit. Don't nobody know I crushed that pussy but you, me and O-Dawg. Everybody else just going off of the word of the streets. Them niggas better stay focused on them Gas Team Niggas and whoever else trying to scrape up O-Dawg's crumbs. Fuckin' wit' us gone get 'em in a casket real quick, and that's on Juice." I spat.

"If my nigga got killed, I'm killin' whoever name pops up first." He tried to kick knowledge.

I placed my hand on his shoulder. "That's the difference between you and them suckaz. We gon' stay on this paper chase. Fuck them niggas."

"I don't like to sleep on niggas."

I didn't either and I knew my nigga was spittin' the ghetto gospel straight from his heart. I knew a whole lot of real killaz that lived in the cemetery now due to them sleeping on the next nigga. That was a cardinal sin in the field, and I knew it.

"You right. It's just that I don't respect their come-up not one bit. When O-Dawg was out, them suckaz were hiding in the house while their homies were getting spanked. Now all of a sudden, they're Bravehearts and talkin' 'bout they run the town. Ace and Flocko are bitches in my book."

"How many niggas we know done turned hard over night? Going up against them Mob niggas was a tall task that nobody coulda won. We gotta look at what they're doing right now, and that's killin'."

I knew he was right like a muthafucka, but for some reason I just couldn't give them pussies no credit. Plus, I felt like deep down inside they knew not to try me.

Ring! Ring! Ring! My phone saved me from having to admit to some bullshit. I pulled my iPhone out of my pocket then slapped my forehead when I saw it was my bitch calling. "I'm almost there, baby." I answered the phone with a lie.

"Whatever, Juice, just hurry up and get here. I'm tired of all these broke niggas and tricks asking if I need a ride."

"I'm almost there, Naughty."

"Bye." She hung up with an attitude.

"I gotta go pick Naughty up from the club. I'll tap-in tomorrow."

"A'ight, Blood. Murda Gang." Gunna replied then tried to shake me up with the 'B' like I was a Blood.

I yanked my hand back like I always did when he tried that shit. "Murda Gang all day, but you can keep that blood shit to yoself. You know I don't like slobs or crabs." I smirked at him.

"You lucky you my brotha or I'd smoke yo ass."

I grabbed my duffle bag off his couch. "Yeah, whateva, lil' nigga." I made my way to the front door.

"I should shoot you in the back, bitch."

"Then who gon' watch yours if I'm dead?" I turned around to him smirking at me. I smirked back then walked out.

I gripped the heat on my waist as I walked through his parking lot. Niggas in the Rockwoods knew not to play with us, but it was always somebody willing to die in the streets over some money. The air was cold and the lot was empty, but I was more than ready to heat it up over these dead white people. I hopped in the truck without incident and peeled out to go pick my bitch up. I had to let up off the gas when I remembered the dope and money in the bag. I couldn't stop the smile from spreading across my face. Just the thought had me showing all thirty-two. I knew shit was about to get back on track for me. Either that or I was gonna have a packed ass funeral.

Marcellus Allen

Chapter 2
Juice

It was only a few cars left in the parking lot by the time I got there. I spotted her homegirl, Jessie's lil' ass Benz and parked next to it. I could see them in there choppin' it up like I didn't even exist. "If this bitch don't come on." I spoke out loud like she could hear me. I told myself she had until the Youngboy NBA song went off to get her ass in the truck or I was gonna drag her out. The song went off and they were still having a fuckin' tea party on my time. "I'm out here takin' penitentiary chances and she wanna sit around gossiping with her stripper friends." I mumbled while hopping out. I yanked the passenger door open, ready to pull her out by the arm until they busted out laughing at me. "What y'all bitches laughing at?" I spat.

They started laughing even harder. "Bitch, I told you I know my nigga!" Naughty bragged to Jessie.

"Yeah, bitch, you was right." She could barely get her words out. "Hey, papi?" She smiled at me.

"What's good with you, Jess?" I replied really not feeling either one of them.

"And, bitch, what did I tell you about calling my nigga Papi? Yo ratchet ass been out of Cuba for twenty years, so cut the shit."

"Whatever, thot."

They could've did that shit all night, but I was running out of patience. "Y'all can do this shit on the phone. Naughty, come on." I helped her out before she could say anything else to prolong the situation.

"I'll call you tomorrow, bitch. Bye, Papi!" Jessie yelled as I slammed the door.

I damn near drug her to the truck before she yanked out of my grip with an attitude. "Why the fuck are you twisting and pulling on me like I'm some type of dog or somethin'?" She folded her arms like all black women did when they got serious and raised her voice.

I sucked in the cold air real deep then slowly blew it out. I'd been rockin' with her for two years and knew exactly how to handle her. I already knew if I flashed on her ass like I really wanted to then we was gon' be arguing in front of the strip club all night. The last thing I needed was for some nosey muthafucka to call the pigs while I had all that hot shit in the whip. I took a quick second to calm my frustration. While I did that, I took her crazy ass in.

Naughty was the baddest bitch working at the Golden Dragon Strip Club by far. She was light skinned, stood about five foot five, had shoulder-length hair and ass for days. She was one of those bad bitches you had to look at two or three times when she walked by. She was a real loyal street bitch, but her feistiness and smart mouth got on my fuckin' nerves sometimes.

"Just get in the car. I ain't got time for this shit right now." I replied.

"Oh, you ain't got time for me? Well, where the fuck you been, 'cause you sure as hell wasn't here on time?"

I ignored her lil' tirade and hopped in the truck. I loved her to death, but she was gon' fuck around and get left. I opened the door and told her to get in or get left. She took her sweet time but eventually got in and slammed the door. I turned on Finesse2Tymes then peeled out the lot. I let my nigga spit the ghetto gospel through the speakers while I was deep in thought about my next moves. It didn't last more than five minutes before Naughty turned the music off. I wasn't trippin' though, it was expected. She hated being ignored just like any other woman on this earth.

"Why were you so late and why the hell you got some type of attitude? And you bet not have been with no ratchet ass bitches either." She leaned against the door staring me down.

I was too sparked about the money to beef with my bitch, nor did I have the energy to. She always thought I was out with another bitch, but I couldn't blame her 'cause I stayed cheating on her. I exhaled. "I'll show you." I grabbed the bag off the backseat then dropped it on her lap. I spoke while she examined the contents. "That's what I've been doing all night, trying to get shit right for us. I almost lost my life tonight for that shit." My mind instantly flashed to me dropping to the floor in the nick of time and bustin' my heat. I shook the thought away. "I had to crush a nigga for everything you see in that bag. So, when I tell yo ass to hurry up and get in the car, trust it's for a reason." I spat.

"I'm sorry, daddy, I didn't know." She kissed me on the mouth, then started counting the money again.

"Do we needa pick up Jamar from ya mama's house?"

"No, he can stay the night over there. Are you staying the night with me or are you going home?"

"I'ma stay with you."

Naughty stayed in some top-notch condos downtown and I had a bachelor's pad on 15th and Freemont, right in the heart of North-East. Wasn't no way in hell that I was driving across that bridge again with that hot ass pistol on me.

Once we made it inside, I collapsed on the living room couch exhausted and thankful that I'd dodged the grim reaper once again. I was only twenty-one but felt like I was fifty. *These streets a make a young nigga feel old.* Jay-Z said it the best.

"Daddy, you want me to run you some bath water?"

I looked over at her like she'd lost her damn mind or something. "Hell naw, I ain't takin' no fuckin' bath. I'ma real street nigga and you know that. Shit, next thing I know you gon' be trying to shave my legs and shit." I was dead serious.

She busted out laughing. "Taking a bath doesn't mean you're not a real nigga, Davontae."

"I'm cool on the bubbles. You can hold that. But I do got somethin' you can do for me."

"What is it?" she asked.

"Log on to ACCESSCorrections and send O-Dawg an email for me with some pictures too. Give him my line and tell 'em to hit me. Matter of fact throw a couple hundred on his books. His government is Marshawn Anderson."

"Boy, I know his real name. Who the hell don't? And I don't know why you wanna put money on his books. Shit, he probably got a million on there already." She replied while pulling her phone out and logging in.

"'Cause that's my nigga and I wanna do somethin' for him myself. You know everybody forget about you when you go to jail."

"Shit, not him. He stay having these dumb hoes arguing over

him on his Facebook." She sat the phone down on the table then stood up. "I'ma go run my bath then I'll take care of all that for you." She disappeared down the hall.

I grabbed the bag and headed to the bedroom where I kept a small safe. I opened it and stared at the lil' ass stack that was staring back at me. Usually I'd get depressed just looking at the measly five-thousand dollars. "I brought you some company." I spoke to the money like it could hear me. With each stack I transferred into the safe, I felt more and more of a rush run through my body. *Bitch ass niggas tried to stop me from eating.* "Baby, how many pills did you move tonight? And how much did you make altogether?" I yelled at Naughty.

"I don't know how many, but I sold a nice amount tonight. It's probably close to three bandz altogether with my tips. Grab it out my purse and count it!" She yelled back.

Tonight was a good night for both of us. Damn, I love my bitch, I thought while I did a quick count of the total amount we'd brought in. I put the brick in the safe last, then closed it with a smile on my face that was usually a rare appearance.

I stripped down to my boxer-briefs in front of the mirror and took myself in. My dreads hung down to the bottom of my neck, giving me that savage-street nigga look. I was barely 170 pounds soaking wet and stood 6 foot 3. Tattoos covered damn near every inch of my brown skin, including my face. I stared into my eyes and saw nothing but blackness and an untamed desire to win at all cost. A thirst for revenge that was unhealthy, but necessary to keep me breathing. I wasn't leaving the earth until I killed the nigga that killed my brother. *Freeze.* Just saying his name made me wanna go kill somebody. I hated him that much. I held up my brother's chain and zoned out.

7 Years Earlier

"A'ight, lil' nigga, take yo ass in the house and don't say nothin' to mama about the fight either." Juice told me after pulling up to the house. It was summertime so he was able to convince mama to

let me go to a house party with him. But like most parties in the hood, it got shut down early 'cause niggas started fighting and gangbangin'. One minute everybody was dancing, then the next, my brother and his Blood homies were stomping some nigga out.

"I ain't gon' tell mama nothin'. I ain't no snitch." I spoke from the heart.

"Good, keep that attitude til' death calls yo name. Never snitch, never betray yo niggas."

I nodded like I always did when he dropped jewels on me. "I know, big bro. Here." I took off his customized chain to hand it over. I was honored that he'd let me rock it outside of the house.

"Naw, go ahead and hold it down for a couple days. Let the bitches see what a real nigga look like with ice around his neck." He said with a smirk on his face.

I didn't know what to say, I was speechless. Our mother walked onto the porch before I could say anything, and we both knew what that meant.

"A'ight, bro, love you." I tossed the ice back on then shook him up with our signature shake.

"Yo, lil' nigga." He stopped me right before I closed the door. "If you let a nigga lift that chain off yo neck, don't ever speak to me again unless it's behind the jail glass or at yo funeral. You better be willing to kill or die behind that medallion." Even though I was only 14 years old, he meant every word that had come out of his mouth. He didn't tolerate no type of coward shit around him.

I nodded then made my way up the steps. "Hi, mama." I greeted her.

"Hey, and what you doing with that stupid chain on, boy?" She looked me up and down, not approving of the look. Her eyes quickly transformed to pure fear. "Juice!" She screamed.

I spun around and saw a nigga closing in on Juice's passenger side. The ski mask on his face and pistol in his hand let me know what time it was. I tried to scream my brother's name, but the shock wouldn't let me, plus it was too late.

Boom! Boom! Boom! Boom! Boom!

My mother tackled me to the floor, but my eyes never left the *shooting. I saw my brother's body slump across the wheel while he ate the bullets one by one. I watched his blood spray all over the window. Then it was over. The killer hopped into the backseat of a waiting car and peeled out. My mother never stopped screaming as she ran to the car.*

"Juice! Juice!" Naughty snapped me out of my flashback.

"Yeah, what's up, baby?" I hurried up and wiped away the tears that were building up in my eyes.

She shedded all her clothes and was down to her bra and thong, looking like one of them video vixens. She walked over and wrapped her arms around my neck. "Were you thinking about your brother again?" She asked, then started nibbling on my ear.

I palmed her ass then kept it real with her. "Yeah, but I'm good now. I can't wait til' that bitch ass nigga get out." I was getting heated again.

She slid her hand in my briefs and started massaging my dick. "You'll get him, daddy, but right now I need you to get this pussy." Her tongue found its way in my ear and I eventually gave in to the feeling.

We started kissing and feeling on each other, heating our bodies up. She dropped to her knees then yanked my briefs down. My dick was as hard as a missile and was poking her right in the face. She licked it from my balls all the way to the head, then stuffed it down her throat. "Aggh shit." I moaned, then gripped the back of her head. *Sluupp! Sluup!* She sped up the pace, making the room sound like a porn scene. She moaned and kept eye contact with me the whole time she swallowed the meat. I leaned my head back and rolled my eyes as I felt my nut getting ready to explode. "I'm about to bust!"

"Bust then." She demanded with a mouthful of dick.

"Agghh! Shit!" I shot a load of nut in her mouth while I gripped both sides of her head.

She sucked and pulled it out inch by inch until it was back poking her in the face. Then she stuck her tongue out, letting me see all my nut on her tongue, then slowly swallowed all of it. *Got-damn.* "Come fuck me in the bath now." She demanded then walked off with all that ass clapping at me.

The Streets Stained My Soul

I followed right behind her with my dick in my hand.

Marcellus Allen

Chapter 3
Juice

A few days later I stepped out of my house with a thousand things to do, but not enough hours to get it done. It's crazy how when a nigga got a lil' money to spend, all of a sudden his schedule got packed. I have shit to do. Broke niggas stayed at home all day playing Madden on the couch and shit.

It was hot as hell outside, especially for mid-February, but I took it as a sign from the game gods that it was my time to shine. I pulled up to my baby mama Brittney apartments in South-East Portland twenty minutes later. I hadn't seen my youngest daughter Ashley in a few days, so I needed to tap in with her. Plus, I needed to drop some change off on Brittney. It had been over a month since the last time.

I used my key to walk in, and the smell of breakfast being cooked attacked my nose and made my stomach growl. "She a good bitch," I said to myself as I made my way to the kitchen. I called her soon as I got up to tell her I was about to come through and she got up and cooked for a real nigga. She was a cool bitch like that— no drama or none of that sucka shit. She had just started college when she got pregnant with my seed, but she didn't let that stop her. She kept on going until she was nine-months, had my daughter, then got back to it. "What's up, baby girl?" I caught her at the stove with some lil' ass booty shorts on and a bra to match.

"Hi, baby!" She was all smiles as she walked over and started tonguing me down.

"You got a fat ass, Britt." I stuck my hands in her shorts, palming both of her cheeks.

"Hmm, you need to do something with it." She purred in my ear.

"I got you tonight, baby. I got hella moves to make right now. What? Yo lil' girlfriends' tongues ain't been getting the job done?"

She rolled her eyes. "Don't play. You know ain't nothing like dick from baby daddy. Don't none of them bitches compare to you, and you know that. Speaking of such, you know this my last year in school, right? I graduate in a few months, and you know what that means."

"Aww, shit," I whined. I knew exactly what it meant and what she was getting at. "Yeah, I know what it means, baby mama."

"Alright, I don't wanna hear nothing when it's time, Davontae. I gave you four years to do whatever you wanted and to get yo shit together. So, when that time comes, be ready to make a decision and stick with it. Either you wanna be a family man with me and your daughter or you don't."

I slapped myself on the forehead out of irritation. This was the only thing in the world that Brittney nagged about. She knew I was a young thug when I met her and had no intentions of slowing down, so she gave me until she received her master's degree to figure my shit out. At the time it seemed like some cool shit, especially since I was still stuck on my first baby mama Latoya. But ever since the deadline got under a year, I realized the shit wasn't for me. *Fuck that!*

"Here. This for you and Ashley." I pulled out two stacks from my pocket and handed it over.

"Umm-umm, thank you." She knew I was done with the conversation.

"I'ma go get my daughter." When I walked into my daughter's room, she was so caught up in one of her movies that she didn't even notice me standing there. I stared at my beautiful baby girl with her doll in her hand and tried to picture being a family man. I loved my kids more than life itself but having a lunch box and hard-hat just wasn't for me. I would hate for my babies to be raised with me in a coffin, but the least I could do is leave them a million apiece. I shook the thoughts of death out of my mind and approached my baby. "Ash-ley!" I sung her name.

She spun her head in my direction. "Daddy! Daddy!" She screamed her head off then climbed down her bed, running straight to me.

"Hey, baby girl." I lifted her up then planted kisses all over her face. "C'mon. you ready to eat breakfast with mommy?"

"Yup!"

I took her to the table and played with her until Brittney sat our plates down. "Thank you, baby mama."

"You're welcome, baby dad. And thank you for coming to spend family time with your real family." She shot back with a lil' heat on her words.

I knew she was referring to me always spending time with Naughty and her son. And it didn't help that Naughty stayed posting videos and pictures of the three of us together. I got up and grabbed her arm. "C'mon, I know what you need." I pulled her up then looked at my daughter. "We'll be right back, baby. Eat your food and don't make a mess either."

"Okay, daddy."

I pulled her all the way to the bedroom and bent her over the bed. I yanked those booty shorts down, slapped her fat ass, then pounded her out from the back until she tapped out with a whole other attitude.

After I handled my business with Brittney, I jumped in the truck and headed out to Vancouver, Washington to go see my oldest daughter Lisa. Her mama Latoya was my original Ryde-or-Die bitch since grade school, but she became the definition of a woman scorned. Once I got Brittney pregnant only a year after Lisa was born, the relationship turned to shit. It got to the point where I had to pull pistols on her family just to see my daughter.

It took a lil' over thirty minutes to cross the bridge that separated Oregon from Washington, then pull up to the townhouse that Latoya lived in. I inhaled deeply then let it out. I had to mentally prepare myself for the crazy bitch. It was never no telling what kinda mood her bipolar ass was in. I knocked on the door and waited. I could hear her yelling.

"What's going on, Davontae?" She answered with an attitude like I didn't call her hours ago.

Here we go. "Shit, what's good? I got the money for you like I told you earlier. Can I come in and see Lisa, or are you gonna bring her out here?"

She was blocking the doorway like she didn't want me coming in. "Oh, my bad, come in. She's back there in her room doing God knows what." I couldn't help checking out her cakes jiggle in those leggings she had on as she walked in the house.

Her other baby daddy Rocky was sitting on the couch, staring at me stare at his bitch's ass. I didn't give a fuck though. That nigga knew I'd fucked her in all three holes a thousand times. Their son was almost a year old and I didn't care for either of them. Even though we weren't together, that bitch knew better than to have another nigga's seed, especially a son. The shit boiled my blood so bad that I hadn't even fucked her since she was a few months pregnant. According to her, the nigga claimed we were still fuckin' and brought it up every argument.

"What's up, homie?" I decided to respect him in his own house.

"Arguing with this crazy bitch." He growled.

"Who the fuck you talkin' to like that? Oh punk ass nigga! Coming in here at eight in the morning like I'm some weak ass bitch or somethin'." She flashed on him.

I noticed he still had on his outfit from the night before, shoes and all. I shook my head and let out a light laugh. "This for you and my daughter." I pulled out all ten-thousand I had in my pocket just to stunt, then handed her two stacks.

"Thank you."

"You good, you ain't gotta thank me for doing what I'm supposed to do. We're still family, you have my daughter." I could see the love and appreciation in her eyes. I could also see the envy and jealousy in her nigga's eyes.

When I walked off, she started diggin' in his chest again. "If you gon' come home at eight in the morning, at least bring some fuckin' money in, broke ass nigga!"

I laughed to myself as I ran up the stairs to my daughter's room. When I walked in, she was sitting on the bed covering her ears. "Daddy!" She got hella excited when she realized it was me.

"Hey, baby," I scooped her up and planted kisses all over her. "You okay, sweetheart?" I could see the sadness in her eyes.

"Mommy and Rocky keep yelling at each other."

I didn't know what to say to a five-year-old about the shit so I changed the conversation. "Have you ate yet?" She shook her head.

"You wanna hang out with daddy today?"

She started screaming, "Yes," and was all smiles. Seeing her that happy to be with me brought a smile to a young killa's face. The whole time I helped her get dressed, I could hear them yelling and getting louder by the minute.

"Where the hell you think you're going with my daughter?" Latoya turned her attitude toward me when we made it to the living room. They were standing in each other's face when we walked in, now they were facing us.

I had to remind myself she was going through it. 'Cause she knew I didn't go for that yelling shit or playing with my daughter. "First off, lower yo tone when you're talkin' to me 'cause I ain't ya nigga. Second off, she ain't yo daughter, she's *our* daughter. Our daughter is hungry so I'm taking her to get some food and spend time with her sister. Plus, y'all doing all this yelling and shit in front of my seed. Got her back there covering her ears up. Y'all got some shit to figure out and she don't need to be here while y'all do it." I spat.

"Nigga, don't try to make me sound like a bad mother or somethin', like I don't feed *our* daughter." She shot back.

"Never that, Toy-Toy. You're a great mother. I'm just gon' take her for a few hours while y'all figure y'all shit out." My compliment wiped the aggressive look off of her face. But her nigga looked like he had a problem.

"Fine. Just bring her back before her bedtime." She gave in.

While she hugged our daughter goodbye, I looked Rocky in the eyes and wasn't feeling what I saw at all. "What's up, my nigga? You look like you got somethin' to get off ya chest." I threw the challenge out there.

"As a matter of fact, I do," he shot back then poked his lil' chest out. "I ain't feelin' how you came at my bitch, first of all, and what you mean, you ain't her nigga? It sound like you was trying to shoot a shot at me." Envy was dripping from every word he spoke.

"Hold that thought." I spat back, then took my daughter to the truck.

Every second it took me to strap her in, the madder I got. I

31

slammed the door then rushed back to the house. They stared at me the whole time, not knowing what to do. The fact that he let me walk away like that and then come back let me know he was a real bitch. A real nigga would've went and got his gun. I walked right up in his face. "Talk that gangsta shit now and say it how you just said it, too. On my dead brother, I'll put yo brains all over this furniture right now." I growled with my hand right on my hip. The .40 cal was calling my name. I didn't pull heat out unless somebody was dyin' fo'sure, and if he said the wrong word he was dyin'.

"Man, you better get out my face." His tone was way turned down.

"Or what, nigga?" I took a step closer.

"Juice, stop! Just take Lisa and leave." Latoya tried to save him.

I didn't budge one bit. I kept my pupils locked on his for a few more seconds. We looked like one of those pre-fight boxing stare downs. I could see all the pussy running through his veins. I was a shark that had just smelled blood. Their son started screaming from his room when I was about to slap the shit out of him. He must've felt his father's soul getting ready to depart from the earth.

"Go get Lil' Rocky!" Latoya ordered him.

He walked off like he was hard, but we all knew he was more than happy for the excuse to leave.

"You a trip." She said with a smile on her face after he was gone. She enjoyed the shit.

I mugged her then walked out the house.

Chapter 4
Juice

I hung out with my baby girls until the sun went down and they were knocked out in their seats. We went everywhere— to the mall, the arcade and even out to get ice cream. I had a whole lot of other shit to do but most of it got rescheduled, 'cause seeing the looks on my angels' faces were priceless. I dropped off Ashley with no problem, but when I pulled up at Latoya's it was an issue. She asked me to start staying in the car whenever I picked my daughter up for a while. I guess her soft ass nigga didn't want me in the house but didn't have the heart to tell me himself.

"It's just for a lil' while until y'alls tension die down." She had the nerve to say with a straight face.

I looked at her like she was the scum of the earth then peeled out without saying a word. There wasn't shit to say as far as I was concerned. She chose a pussy nigga over me, but I wasn't about to stress over a bitch that didn't belong to me. I had money on my mind.

"Yo, I'm ready to link up. What's good?" I hit this D-Boy nigga I knew named Pistol Pete.

"A'ight, meet me at Faith's house in like thirty." He replied.

"I'm on the way right now." I hung up confused on why he wanted to meet at her spot.

It took about ten minutes then it hit me. He wanted to meet at Faith's, who was Naughty's gold-digging ass best friend, 'cause he thought it was a safe zone. He must've figured that if I was on some grimy shit that I wouldn't kill him over there. Real killaz didn't leave behind a witness that could point them out later on. So, if I killed him I would have to smoke her too. But according to his logic, I wouldn't crush my bitch's so-called sister 'cause it would crush her too. But he made a deadly miscalculation. I didn't give a fuck about her trick ass. She stayed hatin' on me to Naughty, trying to destroy what we'd built. I'd lost count how many times she'd snitched on me for being with another bitch.

If I was on some foul shit, I wouldn't let no bitch stop my

money. I'd split both of their wigs then provide Naughty a shoulder to lean on at the funeral. Lucky for him I was on the up and up and didn't believe in robbing or killing anybody that did good business with me. Pistol Pete never played dirty with me, so I had no intention on throwing mud on him. I had a brick of soft sitting in a backpack in the back of the truck with his name written all over it.

I pulled up to Faith's house in the suburbs of Beaverton that I knew some trick nigga cleared out his safe for. Faith was a bad bitch, but I wish the fuck I would give any bitch my hard-earned money. Fuck that.

Pistol Pete opened the door rockin' some hoop shorts, a hoody and had a newly sparked Backwood in his mouth. "What's crackin', Cuz?" We shook hands then posted up on the couch in the living room.

"You already know; trying to get to this bag." I replied while accepting the weed from him.

"Hey, Juice." Faith walked in looking like an Instagram model.

"What's good, big sis?" I laid the love on thick.

"About to get up out of here and meet up with the gang so we can go shopping."

I bet y'all is. I laughed. "I got Naughty's Lexus out the shop and now y'all wanna ride through the town three cars deep, huh?"

She smiled at that. "And you know this," she responded then sat on Pete's lap. "Daddy, you need me to do anything for you before I leave?"

"Naw, baby, I'm good. Go do ya thang." He stuck his tongue in her mouth then let her up.

"See you later, Juice." She walked by.

"A'ight, sis." *She got a fat ass but fuck all that.*

As soon as she walked out I placed the bag on the table and took the brick out. It was time to get to the money, but I just couldn't resist asking him, "Yo, why'd you wanna link up over here? You know my sis got a big ass mouth."

"Shit, I spent the night and didn't feel like moving. I been cooped up all day. Shit, I pay rent in this muthafucka, I might as well get money in it." He started laughing at his own joke.

I just smirked. *You and ten other trick niggas.*

"We good though. That bitch no better than to speak on my business, Cuz." He vowed.

Everything he said went in one ear and out the other. I wasn't going for that shit. Didn't no real street nigga let an outsider know where they rested their head unless it was necessary. We weren't friends, and the pistol poking out of his hoody let me know there wasn't trust either.

"A'ight, that's Gucci. What you think about this work though? Is it butter?" I was done with the small talk.

He took a few seconds to rub the coke on his gums to test the strength of it. He did it once more then nodded his approval with a look of satisfaction on his face. "Yeah, loc, I'ma need this." He nodded again and I could see the dollar signs in his eyes. "Same price like always?" The way he said it made me believe I could tax him a few extra bands, but I wasn't gonna get greedy on him.

"Same price, my nigga." I answered.

He hopped up with a smile on his face. "I'll be right back then."

I moved my hand a lil' closer to the burner on my hip for easier access. I didn't think he would try to play the game foul, but you never knew a man's heart. I'd seen desperation kick in and make the pussy-hearted behave like real life killaz. When he walked back in with stacks of money in both hands I started to relax. *I wonder how much bread he got back there. I should crush his ass.* I had to fight my inner demons and place a smile on my face.

"You ready to get this money or what?" He was way too excited. He dropped the rubber banded stacks on the table then leaned back, getting real comfortable.

I looked at the five separate stacks on the table for a few seconds then swiped them in my bag.

"You not gon' count it?" He asked.

"Naw, we good. I'm sure each stack is five-thousand," Then I grinned at him like a hungry wolf about to devour his prey. "Plus, I doubt you'd ever try to snake me out of my hard-earned money. That would only lead to a bunch of unnecessary body bags."

"I feel the same way, Cuz."

I felt the threat in his tone but chopped it up as machoism. I could respect it, but never would I fear it. I gathered my shit and stood up to leave. It had been a long day and I was ready to get home and count my money, then pass out. "I'm gone, my nigga. I'll holla at you whenever I run across somethin' else."

"I actually got some shit to holla at you about. It's about puttin' some mo' money in ya pockets." The look on his face was one I'd become all too familiar with. The look of death was now in his eyes.

"Talk to me." I sat right back down with the thoughts of money on my mental.

"I got a nigga. Well, actually, two niggas that I want you to smoke for me. But before I tell you who they are, I gotta know do you have a problem with killin' a Red Rag?" His question confused the hell out of me. Everybody in Portland knew I didn't bang no color, so why would I favor their existence over the Crips? Money was money to me, and anybody could get it as long as we didn't eat off the same plate.

"Why would I have a problem? I ain't got shit to do with y'alls color war. Long as we don't grind together then I ain't ever got an issue." I spoke the truth.

"'Cause all yo main niggas are Bloods or Blood affiliates. You was affiliated with them Mob niggas and—" He paused as if he needed to pick his next words wisely. "Your brother Juice, rest his soul, was a Blood."

I could see where he was coming from. "My niggas are my niggas no matter what. O-Dawg fed me, and my brother is dead. I have no loyalty to no color, period." I spat.

He nodded his understanding then stared at me for a full minute, obviously debating if he should he trust me or not. I stared right back at him, showing him there was nothing to hide. I spoke the truth.

"Since yo bro is dead, then you wouldn't have a problem killin' some niggas from his old hood, right?" He finally came out with it.

"The only nigga I can't crush from the Hit Squad is Breeze. Any of his homies can get it though; fuck all them niggas." I let my anger toward them slip out on accident and the look on his face told me he picked up on it.

"Jimmy and Marcell, I want them both dead. They think they can run off with my dope—"

I cut him off with my hand. "The reason don't matter to me, only the price tag."

"Forty thousand for both of 'em, twenty upfront." He shot back.

"They're dead. Now go ahead and grab those twenty bandz real quick." It was nothing else to be said. I didn't like those niggas anyway. They'd been around since the days of my brother and hadn't bodied not a soul behind his name.

Marcellus Allen

Chapter 5
Juice

It was a lil' past eleven o'clock when I made it to Naughty's spot. She was chillin' with her son, Lil' Jamar, in the bed when I walked in.

"What's up, baby? And, Jamar, what yo lil' bad ass doing up this late?" I greeted both of them.

"Hi, daddy." Naughty was all smiles.

"Sup, Juice! Let me get some money, nigga!" His bad ass ran and jumped on me.

I loved the lil' nigga like he was my own son. I'd been the only father figure in his life the last couple years. I put him down on the bed and pulled out a twenty-dollar bill. "Here, lil' nigga. Now, kiss ya mama goodnight and go get in the bed. And hell naw, we ain't reading you no story or none of that soft shit. Real niggas don't do bedtime stories."

He stuck his lil' chest out then dapped me up. "A'ight. I'm gone. Goodnight, Mama." He walked out like a lil' gangsta without even kissing Naughty. We bust out laughing at his antics.

"You gon' make my baby not wanna kiss me no more." She said.

"You know I don't like other niggas kissin' on my bitch anyways." I leaned over the bed and started tonguing her down. When we finally came up for air, I dumped the bag of money on the bed and told her to count it. "It should be forty-five thousand altogether, baby. If it's a dollar short then I'ma go kill that nigga." I instructed. I already knew all the money was on point. I just wanted her to feel like she was needed. Plus, all bad bitches loved counting money, especially their niggas'.

After twenty-minutes of counting she broke the silence. "Jamar is getting out a few weeks early to a half-way house. He called earlier to tell me and Lil' Jamar." She spoke hella fast, all nervous and shit.

I didn't even put my phone down to acknowledge what she said. I was too busy stalking Marcell's Facebook page trying to get a feel of where he was usually posted up. Niggas stayed snitchin' on themselves on social media and didn't even realize it.

"Did you hear me, baby?"

"Yeah, Naughty, I heard you. What you want me to say? You want me to throw the nigga a party or somethin'?" I shot back. I didn't know why I felt salty, but I did.

She crawled over to me, putting her head on my shoulder. "Don't be like that, daddy, I'm just trying to be respectful and let you know. I need for you to tell me how to move as far as me letting him see his son and what-not. Plus, I know how you feel about him ever since that day on the phone."

"I'm not worried about that shit. He was just jail-talkin', mad at the world that he lost his bitch. I'm not gon' take Lil' Jamar's dad from him. Just don't let him know where we stay and don't be all up in his face."

"I would never do that, baby." She vowed.

"We'll see. Just count the money." I brushed her off.

She had a dumb ass look on her face like I was trippin' or somthin' but I didn't care. Just talking about the nigga made me hot, especially since he talked high-power to me on the phone. I had a feeling he was gon' bring drama into our life with his heartbroken ass. Thinking about him getting out of jail made my mind switch to another bitch nigga that was getting out.

I went to the prison website and found the human that I hated more than any other in my life. Alphonso Harris AKA Freeze. I felt my soul darken just staring at his mugshot. I'd never wanted to take a life more than his— the nigga that took my brother from me. Killed my brother in cold blood right in front of my mama. He was gon' pay for that, even if I had to get the lethal injection to do it. I checked his release date for the hundredth time in my life. He was still being released at the end of the year with his good time.

The thoughts of him and Jamar were too much for my soul. The hate started consuming me. I needed to unleash the beast. I hopped up with a purpose, going straight to the closet. I put on a pair of black sweats, a black hoody and grabbed my Scream mask off the shelf.

The Streets Stained My Soul

When I snatched the .45 off the dresser, that's when Naughty decided to speak. "Are you really that mad at me, Davontae? Please don't leave right now." She looked like she was scared of me.

"I'm not mad at you. I got some shit to handle. Don't wait up." I spat, then walked out before she could reply.

***

It took me twenty minutes to get to my destination in North-East. I sat in front of Top-Guns house with nothing but murder on my mind. Top-Gun was Freeze's cousin and co-defendant on his present charges. They'd gotten caught up in a string of shootings and weapon charges and both plead out. Top-Gun got a year less on his sentence and had been out for some months. I'd done my homework on him and knew everything about him that I needed to know. I could've killed him months ago but didn't see the point in it at the time.

But with the angel of death whispering in my ear, somebody had to die, and he was going to be the unlucky contestant. Plus, I wanted to make somebody feel the way I felt. Top-Gun's Benz wasn't parked outside but I didn't let that discourage me. It was past two o'clock in the morning and if a nigga wasn't at home, then it was only one other place he could be. I pulled off, headed right to his bitch's house off of 60th and Killingsworth.

When I pulled up to the duplexes she stayed in and saw the Benz parked by the curb, an evil smirk appeared on my face. *That's yo ass, nigga!* I sat there for twenty minutes trying to come up with a plan to crush him. If he would've been at home I would've pulled a kick-door and it would've been Murda She Wrote. But him being at his bitch's house and me knowing she had two kids, from stalking her Facebook, made that idea obsolete. I wanted to break Freeze's spirit, not make CNN for killing a family of four.

I hit Gunna on the bat-line but he didn't answer. *Nigga probably laid up with a bitch.* I was actually glad he didn't answer after I thought about it. His trigga-happy ass would've wanted to kill the whole house. After giving it more thought, a real wicked game plan struck my mind. I called one of my day one niggas to see if he was with the triv.

After another forty-five minutes of listening to Finesse2Tymes while I watched the house, I peeped a nigga rockin' all black walk by Top-Gun's Benz then stare inside of it. By the way he started looking around it was obvious that he was trying to steal the car. "Look at this nigga." I said to myself. The car thief pulled something from his jacket then started trying to pick the car door and window. It took less than ten seconds for the loud ass alarm to go off. The thief quickened his pace, really trying to get the door open. I saw the lights come on in Top-Gun's spot.

I rolled my window down. "Yo, this guy's trying to steal yo car!" I yelled soon as I saw Top-Gun appear at the door.

"Oh, hell naw!" He roared then took off down the stairs like a track star.

The thief took off down the street and was out of catching distance by the time Top-Gun made it to the street. "Bitch ass nigga, come back!" He challenged.

"You want me to call the police for you?" I held my phone up to my ear.

"Hell naw! Hang that phone up!" He spat like any street nigga would that didn't want the po-po in their mix.

"You sure, man? 'Cause I saw the whole thing." I pulled the phone away from my face.

"Yeah, it's good." He hit the alarm with his keychain then approached the truck. "Good lookin' though, fam. I appreciate you."

"Naw, nigga. Appreciate this." I growled. *Boom! Boom! Boom!* I was out the truck before his body crumbled to the concrete. I stood over him like a pianist but I'm sure to him I looked more like the grim reaper in the flesh.

His hands were clutching his chest in a failed attempt to stop the bleeding while his eyes searched mine for recognition. He wouldn't find it though; we'd never met. His bitch ass bloodline got him sentenced to death.

"Didn't nobody want yo punk ass Benz, Blood." The thief, AKA my nigga Mask, said trying to sound like the nigga from Baby

Boy. He stood over Top-Gun with his heater pointed at his head.

"What I do, fam? I don't even know y'all." Top-Gun moaned through a mouth full of blood.

"Ask the devil when you get there, pussy!" I spat.

Boom! Boom! Boca! Boca! Boom! We made his body do the worm on the concrete from all the lead we filled him up with.

"Ahhhh! Ahhh!" A woman's scream pierced our ears.

Boom! Boom! Boom! Boca! We sent hot shit in her direction, making her run back inside her and Top-Gun's spot. I thought about going to kill her too then quickly changed my mind. I hopped in the truck while Mask ran to his whip. I skirted out with a smile on my face.

Marcellus Allen

Chapter 6
Juice

A week went by and I still hadn't caught Marcell or Jimmy, but I was getting closer, especially for Marcell. He was getting closer and closer to death and didn't even know it. Jimmy was proving to be a lil' more difficult, but I wasn't worried about it. Nobody could hide in Portland forever; the town wasn't big enough. Pistol Pete was starting to get too anxious though and the shit was starting to really piss me off. I could tell that he was worried that I'd fuck him out of his lil' money. I had to check him low-key, letting him know I didn't do dirty business and their caskets would drop in the dirt real soon.

What he didn't know was that I played the house for a few days after crushing Top-Gun to let the heat die down. It was a thousand different rumors concerning his death and a hundred different niggas taking credit for it, but nobody suspected me or my niggas.

"Man, Blood, we need a muthafuckin' play. We need some money, on the gang." Gunna spoke to the whole room.

We were all at my house having a meeting, trying to figure out our next moves. We were just like most Portland cliques when it really came down to it. The love we had for each other was real but niggas were mostly out for self. If I needed one of them to ride shotgun with me on anything, I knew I could count on them, but other than that, niggas just did their own thing. That's how it went in the town. But Gunna, Mask, TJ, Omar and Flash wanted to get more organized, so here we were having another pointless meeting in my eyes. Niggas were gonna walk right out and continue doing them anyways.

"Shit, it look like you and Juice been getting money to me." Omar replied with a trace of jealousy in his tone.

He was referring to the two new diamonds that were hanging from both of Gunna's ears that were shining like a lighthouse. Then to add injury to insult, I was rockin' my new $20,000 Rolex I'd just copped two days before. I hadn't taken it off since the moment I'd left the jewelry store. The diamonds were sparklin' so hard that every time I moved my wrist it looked like a light beam was shooting from my wrist. If they'd known that I'd dropped ten bandz on a bracelet for Naughty too they'd really have a fit. That thirty bandz kinda hurt my safe but fuck it. I was young and getting it, and tomorrow wasn't promised. Plus, I had to bless my bitch for what she was doing for me.

"We went on a job." Gunna told him.

"We went on a job," Omar mimicked him in a deep voice that was supposed to be Gunna's. "Who the fuck y'all think y'all is, Animal Kingdom or somthin'? Fuck out of here."

Everybody started laughing at his halfway joke. It was meant to sound funny, but it was some seriousness in it.

"Which one of y'all niggas is gay ass Darron?" Flash just had to say.

"Man, fuck all that. I need some muthafuckin' money, Blood. Who got the play on some bandz?" TJ spat, sounding frustrated. He was always the serious one out of the group.

"I got somethin' lined up if you wanna ride with me on it. We can split twenty bandz in half." I spoke up.

All eyes were on me now. "Holla at me." He responded.

At first, I was gonna keep the contract to myself 'cause I needed the bread, but hearing how bad my niggas were doing made me feel guilty. "I got somebody paying twenty stacks a head for Jimmy and Marcell's casket. I'm already bakin' a cake for Marcell, but I'll pass one of y'all Jimmy."

Somebody whistled. "Somebody really wants them niggas dead, huh? I gotta collect that." Mask threw his bid in.

Everybody but Gunna started claiming how bad those two were dead. They sounded like they were ready to mask up that very moment. It was dollar signs in our eyes mixed with malice in our hearts.

"Who put the money out?" Gunna growled. It was obvious he felt some type of way.

I hesitated. "Pistol Pete," I whispered, already knowing where the conversation was headed.

"Fuck out of here!" He jumped off the couch in a fit of rage. "We're not about to kill no real Damus for no bitch ass Crab. Let him do his own dirty work. Y'all in here acting like we don't fuck with them niggas or somethin'. Like we don't be mobbin' with them Hit Squad niggas on the regular. And, Juice, you know you out of pocket, Blood. Yo brother helped put Hit Squad on the map and was killed by a Crab!" His fist were balled like he was ready to scrap.

I didn't like how he was staring me down with his chest poked out like he was some type of Suge Knight. Him of all people knew what it was with me. The fear of man didn't exist in my heart. But what really had me seeing red was him trying to use my brother's legacy against me for his benefit.

"Keep my brother's name out yo mouth, nigga!" I roared as I stood up to meet his challenge. "I don't give a fuck about no Crips or Bloods and you know that, so miss me with that Damu love shit. And I really don't give a fuck about no Hit Squad niggas either. How many niggas they body behind my brother? Huh? Shit, me and Mask just bodied one of those Rose City Crip niggas the other day. They should've did that eight years ago! How many niggas in here is Breeze feeding?"

I looked each nigga in the eyes and not one of them could deny my logic. I could see the fire dancing in Gunna's though. I knew he felt some type of way 'cause Breeze was like his favorite cousin, but the truth is the truth. Him and my big brother were best friends but that didn't mean shit no more. I couldn't name one time the niggas done gave me shit for free.

"He still my family." Gunna spat

I shrugged. "You said that to say what?"

"That if we kill his homies and he find out, that he's gonna want blood." He spoke like he was teaching a kindergartener.

"And you said that to say what?" I repeated. As far as I was concerned there wasn't nothing else to be said.

Gunna caught on to what I wasn't actually saying and just stared at me. The tension was getting thicker and thicker with each moment of silence that passed. He had a Napoleon Complex and I had the heart of Wayne Perry, so neither one of us wanted to look away first. I understood where he was coming from as far as his cousin went, but my money was more important. Fuck who ain't like it.

"Yo, y'all niggas fall back on that dumb shit fo'real."

Mask hopped off the couch and got in between us. "We needa be trying to come up with ways for all of us to eat together instead of finding ways to beef."

"I'm about to eat regardless," I stated while I sat back down. "And I don't care how no nigga feel about it either. I'm not gon' starve based on no outsiders' feelings. You lyin' to me."

"Yeah, aight, nigga." Gunna shot back with an evil look in his eyes. After staring me down once more for a few seconds, he walked out the house and slammed the shit out of the door.

If he wasn't my right hand I would've shot 'em in the back of his head for that look he gave me. I'd been in the streets my whole life and knew exactly what that look meant. But we'd been through much deeper shit than this, so I let it slide off my back.

"So, what y'all think?" I had a smile on my face when I asked the room.

***

A few hours after the bullshit, I was having a date with my bitch at Ruth's Chris. I really wasn't the type to get all dressed up and shit just to go eat some punk ass food, but I did it 'cause that's what she wanted. Every Sunday she picked a spot for us to eat. Just me and her spending quality time, working on our relationship and all that other corny shit she liked to preach.

"I love when you dress up. You look like a sexy ass thug in a suit and that always make my pussy wet." She said in a sensual tone then bit her bottom lip.

"I am a thug in a suit." I brushed the invisible dirt off my blazer with a cocky smirk on my face. "Naw, I'm just playing, baby. You look hella beautiful right now, like always."

"Umm-hmm, that's what I thought, nigga. Recognize a bad bitch when you see one." She flipped her hair over her shoulder like them diva bitches. That made us laugh.

"I got somethin' for a bad bitch." I pulled out the Tiffany's box from my jacket and placed it on the table. The smile on her face was priceless. "Here. Let me see yo hand." I put the iced-out bracelet on her wrist then kissed her hand. "Now you got some new ice to go with that new sexy ass dress you got on." I told her.

"Thank you, daddy." She showed a nigga some love by sticking her tongue down my throat. Then she held her arm up, examining all the diamonds. "Next time, don't make me wait so long, nigga."

I screwed my face up, confused. But she spoke up before I could speak my mind.

"Oh, you know better than coming home rockin' a new expensive ass Rolex without coppin' a real bitch something. I ain't no middle of the mall type of bitch and you know that, shit." She paused to stare at the diamonds glistening in the light. "But you did good by choosing this one. Thank you."

All I could do was shake my head at her feistiness and conceit. I couldn't say shit 'cause she spoke the truth like a muthafucka. She was a thorough street bitch that played her role better than any other bitch I'd ever had. She knew her worth and I did too. We were a perfect match.

"Are you guys ready to order?" A cute lil' white waitress interrupted our moment.

"Yeah, we are."

I ordered for us then sat back and listened to her tell me all about her day. I nodded every few words, acting like I was really paying attention to her ass. When our food finally came, we dug in like we hadn't eaten all day, which I hadn't. Once I finished my steak, I got to the topic that I really wanted to know about.

"What's up with ole' boy? Is he ready to hit the pussy, Katrina?" I asked, using her alter ego name.

"Yeah, he ready. Look." She pulled her prepaid phone out that I'd bought her just for this purpose.

It took me a few minutes to read through all the texts and look at the lingerie pictures. I peeped how in all the bust-downs, she never showed her full face, if at all. I made a mental note of that shit for the future. If a chick sent me flicks with the face not showing, I promised myself to cut her off. Shit, I was liable to pop her ass. *Dumb muthafucka don't even know what he got coming.*

"Tell me how it all came together, 'cause we can't have no slip ups," I asked while re-reading the texts.

She sucked her teeth which made me look up at her like she'd lost her damn mind. Right before I could check her ass, she started speaking. "I did it just how you told me, Davontae. It's not hard to get a nigga's attention. I do it every night." She made one of those 'Duh' faces like it was supposed to convince me.

"Give me the details." I needed to be one-hundred percent sure she'd done everything right. We couldn't afford for the enemy or the police to put the pieces together now or later.

"I found a bad bitch that live way out in New York, copied her pictures, then made the account. I kept posting new pictures until I got his attention, which was hella fast. We kept liking each other's pictures until he finally slid in my DM. He think I just moved here for school and he wide open. I did it just like you said. And where you get this catfish shit from anyways?"

I smiled and nodded the whole time she gave me the details. *Niggas can't fuck with me; they playin' checkers.* I stroked my gangsta ego and envisioned the look on his face when he saw the devil instead of a bad bitch. "I got it from watching Catfish, baby girl."

Her phone started ringing in my hand as I spoke. I handed it over without looking on the screen. I never clocked my bitch pussy or whereabouts. I'd learned from the streets that a bitch was gon' do whatever she wanted, no matter how many times you called or stalked her. Either she was one-hunnid or she wasn't.

"This him right now, daddy." She told me all excited and shit.

"Tell 'em you gon' hit 'em back." I needed more time to think on how I wanted to play it. My mind raced with ideas as she sweet-talked to mark. I couldn't help but to remind myself that bitches weren't shit unless she was yours. But niggas weren't either, so the playing field was equal.

She hung up with a satisfying smile on her face. "He said he really wants to link up tonight!"

"Naw, tonight ain't gon' work." I didn't wanna rush the job and fuck around and leave evidence for the Boyz. "We'll catch up with 'em in a couple days; make 'em wait for the pussy."

"He claims he's leaving tomorrow night and won't be back for a month. I don't know if that's a trick to get the pussy or what, but he sounded serious."

"Shit!" I pounded the table in frustration. I couldn't afford to let the nigga live another month, nor did I wanna crush him tonight. I told myself I was gon' do him real dirty for making me rush. "C'mon. We gotta leave now. We probably only got a few hours to come up with a game plan." I tossed way too much money on the table then stormed out, determined more than ever to kill a nigga.

Marcellus Allen

Chapter 7
Juice

I was sitting by the window, staring out of it, scoping for the enemy on some real life Malcom X type shit. I had the room pitch dark so nobody could see me from the parking lot, and to match the mood I was in. I had to scramble like Vick to come up with a play but I'd got it done. Lucky for me Mask still had a few months left on his lease from the apartment he'd moved out of months ago. I'd gotten the keys from him then plotted a bitch nigga's demise.

The apartment was completely empty except for me, the 12-gauge in my hands, and the Batman suit I was wearing. Black Nike shoes, black Nike sweats and the hoody to match. Add the Scream mask I had on and that shit equaled my Batman suit. But I didn't tie criminals up and leave 'em for the police to get them. I left 'em splattered on the pavement for the coroner to scrape 'em up.

My phone vibrated in my pocket. The screen lit the dark room up as I read the text message.

He's pullin' up now.

I stared down into the parking lot until I saw bright headlights pull into the spot right below me. I smirked behind the mask when I saw the dead man step out with a dozen roses in his hands. When he pulled his phone out while looking around the lot, that's when I knew it was time to move. I walked out the door then crept down the stairs on some ninja type of shit. I had the gauge leveled with my chest just in case he decided to head up the stairs. If he did, then they would be the last steps he climbed until he went and faced his God.

But I made it to ground level without having to pull the trigga, and there was my target standing in the cold with his back toward me. I crept closer as he held the phone to his ear, hoping to hear a voice I knew he'd never hear again. When he turned around and saw death up close, he did what all bitch niggas did when it was do or die time. He put his hands up and dropped his jaws.

KaBoom! The flame jumped out the barrel and woke the whole complex. He flew into his own car then slid slowly to the pavement with half his chest missing. His phone and a cloud of rose pedals flew into the air.

I walked over to finish my meal. "Don't chase pussy in the after-life, Pussy."

KaBoom! I knocked his face off, doing him real dirty for making me do a rush job. I hopped in the stolen Honda I had parked in the lot and drove smoothly out of the complex. I pulled the mask off and took a deep breath. I felt nothing. No feelings after killing Marcell in cold blood. I thought I'd feel a lil' remorse after crushin' a nigga that used to buy me candy when I was a lil' nigga. But nah, I didn't feel a muthafuckin' thing for his bitch ass. He didn't kill for my brotha so I killed him with no compassion. *Oh bitch ass nigga!* One down, one more to go was my attitude. I already had big plans for the twenty-thousand I was gonna collect after I smashed Jimmy. "Stop hiding from me, Jimmy," I said as I hopped out of the Honda and got in my truck twenty minutes later.

The next day, my mother hit my line while I was rolling up a Backwood. I'd planned on smokin' and sippin' Lean all day in the house, not leaving for shit. I had a rule that whenever I was sippin' I wouldn't leave the house. I'd seen way too many niggas on the ten o'clock news with their faces in their laps from lackin' off the syrup. If those dummies wanted to get killed while they were high that was their business, but not me. I needed to live so I could kill the bitch who killed my brotha.

I finished my weed, put the Lean up then shot to ma dukes' house. I needed to lay low for a couple of days while the streets attempted to indict somebody for the body. But she claimed it was important and needed to talk to me today. I hadn't seen her in weeks anyways. Plus, I had some bread to shoot her.

"What's good, ma?" I gave her a hug and kiss as I walked in her house.

"You feelin' light, boy, you got all these lil' fast girls chasing you and you can't get a home cooked meal?" She said after letting me go.

I rolled my eyes at her then sat down on the couch, getting comfortable for whatever lecture she had prepared for me. I pulled my baby 40. Cal out of my basketball shorts and sat it on the table. The shit was poking my thigh, irritating the hell out of me.

Moms barley even glanced at it as she sat down next to me. She was used to it. She knew I'd become a beast and a lost soul since the moment Juice left this earth. Her favorite saying was she'd rather visit me in jail than next to my brother. I took that shit to the heart the moment the words left her lips. I promised myself that she would never see me in a coffin, but the same couldn't be said for my enemies.

"Where Troy at?" I asked.

"At the hardware store buying some new tools."

Troy was the nigga she chose to marry a few years back. He was cool and I didn't have any complaints about him. Long as he never put his hands on moms then I would stay out of their business and he could keep his life.

"So, what's the triv, mama?" I wanted to get back to my pint of Lean.

"Latoya called me crying about what you did at her house. Why you going over there tripping, Davontae?"

I slapped myself on the forehead. "Man, she lyin' for no reason. Her nigga was trying to play tough so I had to show 'em he was a real pussy. The nigga was mad I was over there pullin' out knots, and he was getting blasted for being broke." I spat, feeling myself get irritated over the lies.

"Either way, Davontae, she said you're not welcome at her house anymore. She's gonna start dropping Lisa off over here from now on. You can pick her up from here and that'll stop all the drama. Honestly, it sounds like she's scared of him."

"Knock it off, mother, she ain't scared of that nigga one bit. She was punkin' him when I got there." I was mad as a muthafucka that she was really playing this sick ass game. I felt like mobbin' over there and pistol-whippin' both of them for testing my gangsta.

"Well, I think he's hittin' her."

"Well, that ain't my problem. She chose her nigga. Long as he don't hit her in front of my daughter, I don't care if he kill her. I'ma show her what happens when she put another nigga over me." I fumed. Every word that came out of my mouth made me get madder and madder. The beast was beggin' to come out.

My mother grabbed my chain and stared at it for a few seconds without blinking. Her mind was with my brotha. It pained me to see her still mourning him. *I'ma kill you, Freeze.* "You act just like your brother did," she told me. I always took it as a compliment when she said that. Juice was my only idol, fuck everyone else. "But you sound like your father right now; tripping over a woman that don't belong to you."

Now that shit made me mad. I looked at her like she'd just lost her mind. "Don't compare me to that pussy nigga, mother. I ain't nothin' like that nigga. He died over a broad while he had a woman and two kids at home. He deserved to die." I spat venom.

"The same could easily happen to you, Davontae. You never know how a jealous man will act, especially when a woman is involved. Let them live their lives; leave them alone." She stared right through my eyes, piercing my soul.

I nodded while getting my anger under control. I knew she was right. My phone went off before I could respond. It was a number I'd never seen before and I almost didn't answer. But something told me to answer it. "Who this?"

"The real king of Portland. The last Mob Boss living." He was the last person I was expecting it to be. But it was him. I knew that voice and arrogance from anywhere. *O-Dawg.*

A smile came to my face. "Nigga, how you calling me like this? You got me on three-way?" I hopped off the couch, hella excited to hear from my nigga.

"I got a cell phone. I'm the Mob Boss, right? This is me. Is that you?"

I busted out laughing. "You got that, you got that. What's the triv, though?"

"I need you to come and see me ASAP. I'm at OSP. Have yo bitch fill out the forms online then come and see me ASAP."

"I'm on it."

"It's some money on the table for you too, lil' nigga. I'm 'bout to go hit this yard and collect some money real quick. Hit me after that's taken care of, Blood."

"I'm on it tonight." I disconnected with a smirk on my face. I knew shit was really about to change for the better fuckin' with O-Dawg. I'd forgotten all about that bitch and her scary ass nigga. My mind was on money now. *Fuck that bitch.*

Marcellus Allen

Chapter 8
Naughty

It had been days since I helped my nigga kill Marcell, but I was still hella paranoid about the shit. I kept reminding myself that this was what I'd signed up for and to deal with it. It wasn't like I was some type of square bitch that hadn't known death up close or somethin'. Shit, my father was on his eighteenth year of a life sentence for a murder. And my lil' brother JoJo stayed poppin' up in the rumor mill for shooting or killing somebody. I'd grown up with plenty of niggas that were now dead and gone. I was no stranger to death.

But I'd never actually participated in killing somebody before. Ever since I saw him dead on the news, my mind wouldn't stop racing about all the possibilities. I made sure I got rid of all evidence like Juice told me to. Shit, I even threw my computer away that I'd used to make the fake profile. I watched way too much CSI to go out like that.

I didn't regret what I did 'cause I did it for my nigga, but I wish he would've warned me. I didn't know he was gonna kill him. I thought it was gonna be a robbery. Then the crazy nigga had the nerve to come in the house and go straight to sleep like nothing happened. That's when I knew all the rumors were true about him. The nigga was crazy. But he was my nigga.

"You okay back there, baby?" I asked my son who was in the backseat playing with his handheld PlayStation.

"Yeah, mama." He replied, not taking his eyes off the game for a split second.

I stared at my lil' man through the mirror and smiled at him. I loved him more than I loved myself and did everything I did for him. I refused to let him grow up without having the best of everything, period. "You ready lil' man? You gon' unbuckle yourself or do you need mama's help?" I asked after pulling up to my mother's house twenty minutes later.

"No! I can do it!" He raised his voice as he struggled to get out of his seat.

Juice got my baby thinking it's wrong to need me. I shook my head when he finally got out and opened the door. The look of determination on his face was priceless. I didn't notice the black charger in my mother's driveway until I got out of the car. I figured my lil' brother copped a new car and came over to show it off. Shit, the way the sun was beaming off of the new paint job I would've shown it off too.

"Your uncle JoJo is here."

"Uncle JoJo? I wanna see JoJo, mama." He said then started ringing the doorbell.

"Boy, stop." I put my key in and opened the door. "Mom, we're here."

"Come to the den!" She responded.

"Where JoJo at? I see he got a new car." I asked when we made it to the den.

Sitting on the couch right next to my mama was the last nigga on earth I wanted or expected to see. I lost my breath for a second while he just smiled at me like he wanted to eat me. He stood up and I instantly noticed all the muscle mass he'd put on. *Damn.*

"Dad! Dad!" My son yelled, surprised, then ran to his father.

I stared a hole through my mother's face. I couldn't believe she had the audacity to let the nigga in without asking me first. The stupid smile on her face was pissing me the fuck off even worse.

"What's up, baby?" Jamar spoke up first.

My trained eye took him in within seconds. He was looking good in a tight-fitted Ralph Lauren shirt that was hugging the hell out of his newfound muscles. He was rockin' a pair of Balmain jeans and some fresh Jordan Twelves. *He looking good.*

"Don't call me that, nigga." I gave him extra attitude then turned to my mother. "And why the hell you invite this nigga over without telling me?" I spat venom. I spun on my heels and walked the fuck away before I said something to her I couldn't take back. I rushed out of the house and almost made it to the car before Jamar grabbed my arm.

"Hold up. Let me talk to you real quick." He pleaded.

"What! What do we possibly have to talk about? You needa be in there talking to your son, nigga."

"I thought you would be happy to see me."

"Well, I'm not, and you shoulda told me you were out. You can't just pop up on me like this! What if my nigga would've been with me? Then what?"

I saw the fire dancing in his eyes. That always happened when a street nigga got angry. He definitely felt some type of way about Juice. Or maybe the fact that I had a nigga in general. "I been out a few days, trying to get my shit together. I'll be out the halfway house in a month or so, then we can work somethin' out. As far as yo nigga go, we'll cross that bridge in due time. Tell homie we needa meet up face to face in the near future." He demanded.

"That's not something that needs to happen." I opened the door and got in, more than ready to get the hell away from him.

He held the door right as I tried to close it. "Let me ask you one more thing before you leave."

I exhaled my agitation. "What, Jamar?"

"Is there a chance of us getting back together?" He asked with a straight face.

"No." I gave him my most serious face. "I got a nigga." I gave it to him raw, crushing his lil' prison dreams.

"What he got that I don't?"

"He doesn't put his hands on me every time he cops an attitude. Or better yet, he doesn't have me start stripping to pay his lawyer fees while he has all types of bitches on the side!" I screamed, then slammed the door in his face. He just stood there looking as dumb as he sounded while I skirted out of the driveway. "Bitch ass nigga!" I yelled out, venting out years of pinned up frustration.

***

"Damn, bitch, he ain't waste no time trying to reclaim what's his!" Jessie busted out laughing.

We were sitting in Faith's front room discussing my newest episode of drama. It seemed like every week at least one of us was going through some type of Love and Hip-Hop bullshit. We were supposed to be out shopping, enjoying ourselves, but were smoking weed on the couch instead.

"Bitch, this shit ain't funny; this some real-life bullshit." I responded to her dumb ass.

"Here, hoe." Faith handed me the much-needed Backwood. I took a couple of deep pulls then tried to relax. "And how the fuck that jail bird come home to some Balmain jeans anyways?" She asked out of nowhere.

That shit had me on my knees crying my eyes out right next to Jessie. We couldn't stop laughing to save our lives. I damn near pissed on myself. Every time I tried to answer her, I ended up laughing even harder, unable to get any words out. I rolled over on my back then took another pull before handing it to Jessie. I finally controlled myself and sat up, looking right at Faith. She was so serious I almost started up again but managed to keep it together.

"Y'all some silly hoes. I was dead serious," she said.

"Bitch, we know, gold-digger." Jessie spoke the truth.

I sat back on the couch, feeling a lil' better after the much-needed laughter.

"Got-damn right, and y'all bitches are too. I just let mine be known from the jump so there ain't no misunderstandings. Niggas gotta pay to play." She shot back. And she was so serious too. My bitch was about her paper, no questions asked. Every broke nigga in Portland already knew not to even waste their breaths. It was pointless.

"Are we gonna talk about breaking niggas, or are y'all gonna help me?" I got back to the task at hand.

Jessie sucked her teeth. "You ain't got no problem, mami. You're just over-thinking it. Yo baby daddy home from jail, that's the usual. You're with Juice now and he gon' have to accept that, end of story."

"Whose dick is bigger, bitch? That's what I wanna know." Faith said out of nowhere.

I slapped my forehead. "What's that got to do with anything?" I was just dying to know.

"'Cause, bitch, I know what the real problem is. You ain't slick. Answer the question."

I didn't even have to think about it. There wasn't a comparison. "You know Jamar got a horse dick." I said with a smile on my face.

"Exactly. You want some of that horse meat, huh? You miss them long-stroke, back-shots, don't you?" Now it was her turn to laugh in my face.

My mind drifted off to his meat and all those crazy positions he used to put me in. When I felt my pussy start to twitch, I knew I had to change the subject. *Do I wanna fuck him still?* My mind said no but my body was telling a different story. I squeezed my thighs closed.

"Naughty, I know you're not thinking of going back to that nigga!" Jessie didn't even try to hide her dislike for Jamar.

"I'm not going back to that nigga; I got one that love me."

"Fuck love. What's that got to do with it? You better hit Jamar's pockets and hit 'em hard. Shit, it sound like the nigga already trying to get to some money. Juice's ass don't deserve the pussy. One minute he on, the next he hittin' you up for dollars. Fuck that shit. His turn is up. Daddy's home."

All I could do was shake my head at the crazy bitch. She always came off as a hater, but I knew that was far from the truth. She was just speaking her truth. She meant every word that came out of her mouth and didn't care how nobody felt about it.

"Y'all hold on, this Pete calling." She held her finger up then answered her phone.

I decided to hop on my Instagram while her gold-digging ass sweet-talked her nigga. The first thing that popped up was my baby daddy. He'd decided to follow me and was posting the shit out of him and our son. I kept scrolling through the pictures and found some from the day before that I knew would be problematic. He had posted a lot of pics of him, Ray Ray and D-Roc. *Aww shit.*

"Pete said to tell Juice to get at 'em." Faith said, bringing me back to reality. She hung up the phone and was staring at me stare at the screen.

"I wonder what him and Pete got going on."

"Oh, bitch, I forgot to tell you!" She got all excited and shit like she had some good tea for me. "Last week, when we went shopping, Juice was over here before I left. Pete had a bag of money for him too."

"I didn't know they were that cool."

"They're not, they just do business together from time to time. And over the past few days, he went from being mad at Juice to being hella excited."

"Mad at him for what?" I really wanted to know.

"I guess he paid him to do something, but it was taking too long. You know how that go."

"Paid him to do what?"

"Bitch, you know what yo nigga be out here doing. Robbin' and killin' people; pick one." She replied in a nonchalant type of way.

But I didn't need to choose one, it had chosen me. *That's where he got the money from.* At that moment it all started to make sense to me. Pete paid Juice to kill Marcell, then he used me in the scheme. I wasn't mad at my nigga but he should've gave me the whole play if he was gonna risk my life. It really made me mad that another bitch knew more than I did about my nigga.

"Pete paid him to kill the nigga Marcell." I blurted out without thinking.

"How you know?" They asked at the same time.

"Don't never tell them messy bitches my business." I could hear Juice's words sounding off in my head. But it was too late, and if he would've keep it real with me from the jump, this conversation would've never happened.

"'Cause I helped him do it." I started feeling better the moment the words left my lips. I needed my girls to help me get over my anxiety. I wasn't cold-hearted like Juice was. He'd have to understand.

Chapter 9
Juice

It was around one o'clock when I'd finally made it through all the metal detectors and all the other bullshit. It was my first time visiting somebody and I was already not feelings the shit. It was way too many steel doors and pigs in one place for me. I kept thinking about all the niggas I'd shot or killed and just knew I'd be arrested at any second. But I was gon' be fly as hell if the Feds were watching, literally. I put all my jewelry on before I'd left the house and had all them CO bitches sweating me. I had on my brother's chain, of course, my iced-out cross that hung damn near to my nuts, Rolex on one wrist and a bracelet on the other. The rock in my ear was blinding every bitch in sight, and my pinky ring was killin' 'em. Every guard that was working and every bitch that was there to visit her nigga couldn't stop staring at me. I was looking like a ball player and they all wanted to be a basketball wife.

"You can have a seat wherever. Your inmate will be here in a minute." A fat ass cracker barked then walked away with an attitude.

I knew his bitch ass was jealous of what he could never be. That put a smile on my face. *Inmate? Bitch ass pig.* It took ten minutes for all the niggas on lockdown to walk in with their creased state pants and long-sleeves. I stood up like everybody else so they could see where to sit. I recognized a few niggas from the streets and gave a few head nods. Walking in last was the person I'd came to see. O-Dawg.

He floated in the room like he was walking in VIP at the strip club. All eyes were on him as he made his way over. My nigga still had that dope boy swag that the bitches loved, and the haters tried to mimic. *How the fuck he got on Prada shoes?* I wondered.

I cracked a smile. "You just had to be last, huh? Just couldn't help it, huh?" I gave my nigga a G-hug.

"This is me. Is that you? The people came up here to see a show. I'm just giving them what they shoulda paid for." His usual arrogance oozed off of his words.

We sat down, trying to get a read on each other. We stared in each other's eyes, searching for any weakness or sign of change. I could see his pain more evident than ever now. I could also see the hate eating away at his spirit. But that's what happens when this dirty game is through with you and spits you out. That's what happens when your main nigga is killed by your homie, then you kill yo homie and your bitch's sister, then yo bitch teams up with yo other main nigga to kill you. Then you gotta kill yo nigga and spare yo baby mama's life just so she can end up killin' yo other baby mama then snitch on you. The betrayal is real.

"Yeah, I see you putting on a show with them Prada shoes on. How the fuck you get them in here?" I asked.

He lifted his kicks in the air so I could get a good look at them. "Millionaires make moves no matter where they're at, nigga; you know that. But fuck all that. You the one in here putting on a show with all that ice on. We know who really getting money." He laughed while he held my arm up to take my Rolex in.

"What's good, though? How you living? Yo kids good?" I asked. The flash of anger I watched ripple across his eyes told me that was the wrong question to ask.

"I'm living as expected, but my kids?" He paused then scooted closer to the table." Lil' Tamia is good, she's way too young to know her Mama's dead, but my son," he growled then took a second to run his hands through his waves. He exhaled then continued. "I haven't spoke to my son since the day I got set up. That snitch bitch won't even let my mama see him. She trying to turn my son against me, Blood." He spat with anger.

All I could do was shake my head and grit my teeth at the foul bitch. Hearing that had my blood boiling like a muthafucka. I felt like going to Latoya's house and shooting her and her nigga just to protect my future with my daughter. *I wish that bitch would play wit' me!* "That's fucked up. I wish I could do somethin' for you, brody." I felt for my nigga.

"You can; that's why your here." His eyes told me what his heart was feeling.

"Holla at me."

"I got seventy-five bands for three heads—"

I instantly cut him off. "Tell me who, when and where, and they're dead. I don't give a fuck who it is." I was already adding the money to my safe by the time I finished my sentence. I needed that bag with a passion, so whoever stood in between that had to die. Simple.

"Good, 'cause I want them all done dirty. Olay, Phatz and Ralo, I want them all dead, on Bloods. You got a problem somin' a bitch?"

"A snitch is a snitch, don't matter if they got a dick or a pussy." I meant that shit from the heart. I'd never snatched a woman's soul from the earth but I knew I wouldn't hesitate or show any mercy. It was way too many real niggas on the chain gang because of some snitchin' ass bitch. They got more passes than these rat niggas did, and they got a lot. But Olay was the worse I'd ever seen and would receive no sympathy from me.

"If her snitch ass wasn't playin' with my son I'd probably let her live just on the strength of him, but she done fucked up now."

"You got a specific dyin' order?" I asked.

Before he could answer, a nigga walked over with a camera in his hand, asking if we wanted to take pictures.

"Let's go flick up for the Gram."

We took a gang of flicks like we were in the club or something. I grabbed a bunch of shit from the vending machine, then we got back down to the business. I left an hour later with a purpose to kill and a plan to add seventy-five bands to my safe. Shit was finally starting to look up for a real nigga.

I hit up Mask as soon as I hit the parking lot to let him know the triv. It was money up for grabs, so I had to put my niggas up on the score. I usually would've hit Gunna first but he was still in his feelings about the Marcell situation. *He better get it together.* Mask told me that they were all at his house posted up. I told him I was on the way and had a money play for the team. I hung up just as I reached my truck and noticed a thick ass chocolate chick checking me out from head to toe. I recognized her from the visiting room but couldn't remember who she was visiting. She was eye balling me way too hard for me not to bag her.

"What's up with it? How you doing?" I asked then let her see me smile for a split second.

"I'm doing fine, how about you?" She showed me all thirty-two.

I walked over to her, killing the distance. "I'm good but I'd be doing better if we got the chance to get to know each other. My name is Juice."

"Juice? Is that the name your mother gave you?" She laughed after asking me.

"Naw, the streets did." I spat. I was getting irritated by her laughter. I knew she was just playing but I didn't play about my name. That was the same thing as playing with my brother.

"Nice to meet you, Juice, my name is Alexis."

"A'ight, so can we swap numbers, or do you have a man?" I didn't care if she had one or not. And by the way my diamonds were shining in the sun, I knew she didn't either.

"Yeah, we can do that." She replied then handed me her phone.

I gave her mine too. "Were you here to see yo nigga?" I just had to ask.

"My baby daddy, but we're not technically together right now."

Sounds good. I knew exactly what that meant. While her nigga was on lockdown, she was gon' give the pussy up whether he liked it or not. I'd never been to the pen, but I knew the code of the streets real good. I also knew a lot of niggas that couldn't stomach the idea of their bitch getting fucked. That's the reason most of these sucka niggas turned state. "What's his name?"

She looked up from my phone with a confused look on her face. "Tony. Don't tell me y'all know each other."

"Never heard of him; you good." I calmed her fears. I really didn't know who the nigga was, but I knew his bitch was out of pocket.

"Okay, well make sure you call me."

"You got that." I started walking away when she called my name, forcing me to turn around "What's good?"

"You look so familiar. Do you rap or something?"

This bitch serious? "Naw, I don't do no rappin', baby girl. I do the shit them niggas rap about." I let her soak in some of the realist shit she'd ever heard then hopped in the whip. I put on Real with Me by Finesse2Tymes and peeled out the lot. *These hoes ain't loyal*, I reminded myself. But niggas weren't shit either so I couldn't complain. I just hoped to never see the pen.

It took me an hour to get from the penitentiary in Salem to Mask's spot way out in South-East Portland. But when I pulled into the lot on 162nd and Sandy, all my hittaz were still posted up outside in the sun like they were slangin' rocks or somethin'. Gunna was sitting on the hood of his Red 750 with his shirt off, really feeling himself. Everybody else was standing in a circle with smiles on their faces while they laughed at whatever was being said. I parked next to TJ's charger then hopped out.

It was early March and the sun was starting to come out a lil' bit more which also meant that niggas would be out more too. Murder Season was coming up in a few months and I was more than ready to crush somethin'. Robbin' and killin' was my bread and meat, and if I didn't hunt I didn't eat.

"What's up wit' it, gang?" I approached my team with our signature line.

"What's good, gang?" Omar replied first then shook me up.

Everybody else followed suit with the same line and shake but I felt a lil' tension behind Gunna's. Not in a hateful type of way, but more so out of irritation. Either way, I knew it was time to address the elephant or one of us would get stampeded by it in the future. To let anger fester in your heart for too long always resulted in death. It was the law of the jungle and of nature. And if anybody was a master of knowing that, then it was me. My anger for my brother's killer literally consumed me. I went to sleep and woke up every day thinking about decapitating his bitch ass.

"What's good with you, gang? What's on yo mind?" I got straight to the point.

"Shit, you tell me. I'm waiting to hear what O-Dawg is talking about. You know you got Instagram going crazy over them flicks you posted."

He wasn't lying either. My notifications had been blowing up nonstop from the moment I'd posted them. O-Dawg must've had the cameraman on his payroll 'cause he passed me the SD card right before I'd left. I posted them all before I left the lot. But I knew Gunna was holding back his true feelings.

"We gon' speak on that in a minute, but first you needa speak on the triv you're feeling. You ain't never been no pussy nigga that held his tongue so don't start now." I spat.

He was the most dangerous nigga I knew by far and always spoke his mind. Wasn't nothing pussy about him at all. I think he knew that his opinion and feelings weren't shared amongst the gang. "Aint nothin' to discuss. You did what you did and now we gotta hope shit don't get real. My relative looked me in the eyes at the funeral and vowed vengance. You know how that shit made me feel, nigga?" He finally spoke his mind.

I understood where he was coming from and could see the conflict in his eyes, but it was what it was. "I feel you, my nigga, but the damage is done. Plus, you know how we rockin', if niggas ain't gang then they in the food chain, period. I know I put you in a fucked up situation but niggas gotta eat, fam. Breeze and them niggas ain't feeding us, and on some real shit, they lucky we ain't been took their plates."

"Real shit." Flash jumped in.

"You my nigga and I don't want us beefing over this shit. I wouldn't touch Breeze on the strength of you, but that nigga Jimmy gotta go. We hungry. Niggas gotta eat, gang." I finished my speech.

When he started nodding slowly, I knew that he'd finally given in. He knew better than most that these streets didn't show sympathy or love. If a nigga wasn't part of your inner circle then he was food. And these streets were so foul that most of the time that shit didn't even matter.

"You right, Blood, I just don't wanna have to look my Aunty in her eyes if her son is dead." He hopped off the car then shook me up like he meant it.

"Hopefully you don't." I wasn't making no promises though. The streets didn't make none to me, so I wasn't gon' make none to them.

"Man, fuck all that. Can we go in the spot and talk money or what? I'm getting too hot. I'm too big for this shit." Omar jumped in making all of us laugh a lil'. He wasn't bullshitting about the heat or his weight. For some reason the sun had forgotten we were in March and had it feeling like June out in this bitch. But that was weird ass Portland weather to the nine. And Omar was a three-hundred-pound bully who hated to sweat or stand up for long periods of time.

"Shut yo fat ass up, nigga. You need to burn some of that fat off anyways." Flash talked shit like always.

"Whatever, bitch," Omar responded then took off his white t-shirt. "I know if I pass out, I'ma knock yo ass out when I wake up."

"Shut up before I take that lil' ass nine off yo waist and slap the shit out of you with it." Flash shot back.

Omar looked ready to pass out with all the sweat dripping down his face. His pistol was poking out from his jeans for the whole parking lot to see. All it would take was for one nosey ass white person to call the boys, and punk ass gang task would have us face down on the concrete.

"C'mon. Let's go inside and chop it up. The shit O-Dawg want us to do don't need to be discussed outside anyways." I spoke up then headed up the steps.

It took twenty minutes for me to break down everything O-Dawg wanted and how he wanted it done. Everybody was with it. From the sounds of it, it was gon' be a race to see who was gon' get the bodies. It was a bag on the line and every killah in the room wanted their piece of it.

"I'm tired of this shit, Blood!" Gunna yelled as he hopped off the couch and started pacing.

Fuck wrong with this nigga? We all looked at each other then back at him. "Tired of what?" I asked.

"Of all this shit! Being fuckin' peasants that's barely making a living. One minute we robbin' niggas for work, then the next we taking hits. One minute we sending bitches, then the next we selling dope. One minute we're on, then we're broke the next week. I'm tired of this shit, Blood!"

"That mean we gotta start stackin' more." I said in a nonchalant way. I felt where he was coming from, but I wasn't all enthusiastic about the shit. All niggas had to do was stack more and spend less. Simple shit.

"How we gon' stack more if we ain't got steady money coming in?"

"So, what you saying, nigga? You wanna start hittin' more lashes or somethin'? You ready to turn up the knob? I'm with whatever." I was more than ready to step this shit up.

"Juice, you not listing to me, Blood." He got more frustrated. He came and crouched right in front of me, staring in my eyes.

"I'm listening, nigga, but you ain't saying shit."

"I'm saying don't none of that shit bring us a steady cash flow, nigga."

"So, what does then? What you got in mind then?" Gunna was always being hella ambitious but never had a plan to execute it.

"Nigga, you got the plug on speed dial and you need to use it. Tell O-Dawg to plug us in." The passion in his voice and the look in his eyes let me know how serious he was.

"Tell 'em to plug us in, huh? Just like that. Shit don't just happen like that and you know that."

"You right, but how many niggas you know got the plugs number in their phone? Nigga, you just visited the biggest dope boy in the town." He shot back.

"He got a point." Flash jumped in.

I looked at the others and they all looked more than interested at what Gunna was spitting. The dollar signs were in their eyes. "He ain't just gon' hand over the plug and you know that. If that's the case, let's just ask Breeze for his."

"I got a plan." TJ spoke up. All of our heads turned toward him in an instant. He was usually the quiet killah type that just went along with the flow. "Tell O-Dawg we gon' crush everybody on his list in exchange for the plug. Fuck killin' for chump change, let's kill for a real bag."

I leaned back and gave the shit some serious thought. It did seem like something that was worth the risk, but I still had my doubts. "So, now y'all wanna be d-boys all of a sudden? Y'all know that come with a whole lot of shit we ain't used to. That's a whole field we gotta master." I felt like my niggas were so focused on the dollar signs that they weren't really thinking about the drama that came with it.

"Shit, we be selling stolen dope all the time. The only difference is it won't be stolen. We street niggas, it ain't nothing in the streets we can't do. You got the power to change our lives, right here, right now." Gunna said then stuck his hand out. "Are we gang or not?"

I stared at his hand for what felt like eternity then looked each one of the wolves in their eyes. *They all want this,* I told myself. "Till death call our name." I gave in and shook his hand. I felt it in the pit of my stomach. I couldn't describe the feeling if my life depended on it. I didn't know if it was a good or evil feeling, but I knew it was there. I could feel it. That handshake would change not only our lives, but the whole Portland underworld. When I gazed through all of my niggas' souls I didn't see nothing but hunger staring back at me. I felt the power in my bones, I knew it was coming.

We chopped it up for hours about our eventual takeover and the riches we would have in due time. We talked about how bad we were gonna do those three snitch bitches for the love of the money. We finally had a common goal that would unite and benefit all of us. The more we planned, the more I felt better about the triv. I couldn't remember the last time we'd all determined to get something done. The dollar signs were in all our eyes now and only a casket could close them.

Marcellus Allen

Chapter 10

"Ohh! Ohh!" Brittney moaned in ecstasy. She was riding the shit out of my dick early in the morning.

"Got-damn, Britt, get this shit!" I growled while I palmed her ass then spread her cheeks open.

She leaned all the way forward, putting her titties right on my face, wrapped her arms around my neck, then went to work.

"Aghh shit." It was my turn to moan like a bitch, but good pussy will do that to a killah.

"Ohh! You like it, daddy?" Then she stuck her tongue in my ear.

She picked her pace up and had our bodies smacking against each other nonstop. It literally sounded like somebody was clapping. "Hell yeah. Aww fuck, I'm 'bout to nut!"

"Wait for me, nigga!" She started bucking even faster and wilder.

All I could do was wrap my arms around her body and enjoy the feeling. Another few minutes of that shit and it was time to blast off. "Here it come!"

"Ohh, I'm cumming too, daddy!"

We started jerking and grinding on each other to the same rhythm. I felt her getting her nut at the same time I was busting mine. We laid there for a minute or two just holding each other, not saying shit. There wasn't a better feeling in the world than nutting in some good pussy while you laid up in it. *I wonder when I kill Freeze will it feel better than this?*

"You got the best pussy in the world, on the gang." I complimented my bitch.

"I'm glad you like it." She started laughing then got out of the bed. "I'ma go get you a towel."

I slapped her on the ass as she crawled over me, then locked my fingers behind my head as I stared at the ceiling deep in thought. It had been over a week since I'd visited O-Dawg and we still hadn't bodied none of those rat muthafuckaz, but we were getting closer by the day. I still was plotting Jimmy's demise but him and those Hit Squad niggas were out for blood. They'd jumped out on a few crews and shot up a couple of streets, but nothing out of the ordinary.

"Here you go, daddy." Brittney came back and started wiping me down with a wet towel.

"Thank you, baby."

"You're welcome."

I hopped up, threw on my briefs, then started pacing the room. I always paced when it was time to organize my thoughts. I couldn't take my mind off of the snitch nigga Phatz. We'd found out the day before that not only did the coward have a food truck right in North-East but it was on the same block as my bachelor's pad. This snitch bitch had his cart right off 15th in the New Seasons parking lot. I passed by his rat cart damn near every day and never thought twice about it. It was over fifty food trucks in Portland and I didn't fuck with none of 'em. I didn't trust a bunch of hood muthafuckaz cooking my food in the back of some dirty ass truck; fuck that. *This nigga gotta be crazy.* He must've thought since he had a few bodies under his belt that he was Superman. He was gon' learn the hard way.

"I'm glad that you've been spending more time over here, baby." Brittney said bringing me out of my thoughts.

"Me too." I replied without really giving it much thought. My mind was on all the millions that were calling my name, but first I had to eradicate Phatz's hoe ass.

"Don't tell me your lil' stripper went back to her baby daddy." She said out of nowhere.

Now that shit got me out of my thoughts in an instant. I stopped pacing and gave her my full attention. I stared at her putting her bra and panties on in the mirror like what she'd just said didn't mean nothing. Like that shit didn't come out of nowhere. It wasn't her style to hate for nothing or start a frivolous argument out of the blue.

"What the fuck is you talkin' about, Brittney? Why the fuck is you talkin' about her baby daddy out of nowhere? I ain't trying to hear that dumb shit." I spazzed on her.

She looked at me like I was tripping on her for no reason. Like she was confused by my response or somethin'. "Why are you getting an attitude with me? I just asked you a simple question, nigga."

"You the one in here asking dumb ass questions about some nobody ass nigga in jail, not me." I shot back.

She screwed her face up. "Wow, I see what the problem is." She grabbed her phone off the dresser.

"Yeah, you." I started putting my pants on, ready to get the fuck up out of there. I wasn't with the arguing shit.

She handed me her phone with an attitude. "That nigga been out of jail. I thought you knew."

My heart dropped immediately. Those were the last words I was expecting to hear. The feelings of betrayal were running rabid through my veins as I stared with hate at all the pictures of Jamar with his son. I kept scrolling through the flicks trying to see if there were any with my bitch. There was none. *Bitch know better than that!* I sat down on the bed and went through the nigga's Instagram page, piece by piece, comment by comment. The more I saw the more I wanted to kill. I kept track of all the times the sneaky bitch liked one of his posts. But when I saw him with Ray-Ray and D-roc that's when I knew shit had just got real. *She know I don't fuck wit' them niggas!*

"How long he been out?" I hissed.

"A month or so, somethin' like that."

"Dumb ass bitch."

"So, she really didn't tell you? That's what happens when you put your trust in stripper hoes. You was probably just some good dick until her real nigga came home." She just had to say.

For some reason her words irked the shit out of me. I knew she was trying to rub it in my face. I already knew if I responded to her that we were gonna end up in a full fledge yelling match. So, I ignored her and grabbed my phone to tap-in with Gunna about the triv.

"What's good, gang?" He answered half asleep.

"Did you know Naughty's baby dad Jamar got out already?" I got straight to the point.

"Yeah, I heard 'bout it. So what? The nigga's a nobody." He

responded.

"'Cause he was talkin' that high-power shit over the jail phone, that's why. What if he would've got the drop on me."

Brittney rolled her eyes at me then walked out of the room. She was mad as a muthafucka but I could care less.

"Nigga, you ain't said shit 'bout it 'till now so I figured the shit was dead."

"I just found out right now that he was out." I admitted.

"Say what? Nigga, you lying to me." His voice got hella loud. He was fully woke now. "Naughty foul, Blood. Why she ain't tell you?"

"I don't know, but I'm damn sho gon' find out. But fuck all that, did you know he was on some Gas Team shit?"

"Fuck naw! Yo, I'm b'out to get up and come meet you. Give me like an hour. And we need to crush that sneaky bitch before it's too late." He hung up before I could reply.

Hours later

"I ain't feeling this shit, Blood. Somethin' ain't adding up." Gunna spat for the tenth time. We were riding around with no destination in mind, just choppin' it up while taking the city in. We'd went over every scenario possible and Gunna still felt the same way.

"I hear what you're saying, but I can't just go kill my bitch just 'cause she didn't tell me her baby dad was out of prison." I replied.

"I know you can't, just give me the word though." He stared at me with malice in his eyes. He was more than serious and I knew it. My nigga was a stone cold killah with no emotions, and not a drop of empathy in his blood. He was what the world got when the streets took your father off the earth and your mother was addicted to the pipe. He came up the foul way and didn't give a fuck about a life if it wasn't gang, period.

"That's why you ain't got a bitch." I shot back.

"Fuck a bitch. All them hoes are disloyal." He spat.

I nodded and went silent. The situation was really fucking with my emotions and I didn't like how it made me feel. I just couldn't see her setting me up like Gunna was saying. My gut was telling me that wasn't the case. Or was that my heart talking? "Let's catch a rat nigga slippin'." I broke the silence as I whipped into the New Seasons parking lot where a few food trucks were parked.

He gave me an evil smirk. "'Bout time you start speaking my language." He gripped the .40 on his lap while he started looking around the lot.

It was broad day, but we didn't give a fuck about that one bit. We had no problem hopping out, slanging iron whenever or wherever we caught an enemy. Especially a rat muthafucka that felt like he could still get money in the hood. The sun couldn't protect a pussy nigga from the grim reaper.

"You know which one is his?" I growled. My kill a snitch-bitch nigga meter had risen to the highest power in the seconds it took me to park the truck.

"Naw, Blood. The bitch just said he had a cart in this lot. Hold up, I'ma call her right now."

"Naw, fuck all that. We 'bout to just bounce out and figure it out on the move. This ole' Alpo ass nigga out here runnin' businesses and shit like he a real nigga while big bro in a cage like a fuckin' animal." My words were dripping with venom that only a thoroughbred could relate to.

"And this shit across the street from yo house." He stated the obvious knowing that shit was gon' piss me off even more.

"I know. I should go in there and grab the choppa and let his snitch ass feel that." My mind started envisioning his body split in half from them AK bullets.

"On Bloods I'm done talkin'." He spat then hopped out with only one thing on his mental.

"Snitch ass nigga." I said out loud then jumped out on some ready to die shit. I lifted my hoody over my head then stuck my hand inside it, gripping the cold steel of the .45. I got in step right behind Gunna as he led us to the cart he had mentally chosen already.

It was the middle of the day, but the sun was barely out, causing it to look and feel like seven o'clock instead of the two o'clock it was. But I planned on making his body feel like July in the middle of Phoenix, Arizona. *I'ma feel 'em up with this hot shit.*

I got madder with each step I took. Gunna chose the food truck with a few people in line. The other one only had one person and he was getting ready to leave. But Gunna was in kill mode so I ain't say shit about it. While we waited in line, I tried to peep inside the truck every chance I got. All I kept seeing was the same nigga at the window. I knew his face but couldn't place it at the time. But I knew we were at the wrong one.

"Yo, where Phatz at?" I asked the nigga when it was our turn at the window.

He screwed his face up. "That snitch ass nigga shit is over there, Cuz. Y'all needa get some of this real nigga food though and leave that rat alone. Tell 'em to show y'all his paperwork, Cuz." The nigga spat with disgust, thinking we were choosing Phatz food over his.

"We ain't come to eat no food, Blood, we came to eat a rat." Gunna checked him. We turned around instantly and headed to the rat's truck. "We should crush his ass too for knowingly letting a rat get money on the same block as him." Gunna fumed.

I felt where he was coming from, but it was a pointless conversation. We'd have to kill over half the town if we were pushing that line. Plus, I knew Gunna was trippin' 'cause ole' boy was Crippin'.

"I'm killin' this rat bastard soon as he put his head through the window, I'm telling you right now."

"That's the plan." I didn't feel like talking no more, I was in goon mode. I walked up to the window then pulled my heat out, keeping it by my waist so it couldn't be seen.

As soon as she turned around and saw me, she froze up in fear. Her eyes got wide and her hands dropped to her pregnant stomach. I was surprised at who was standing there.

"Anna? What's good with you?" I put a fake smile on my face. We grew up on the same block and her big brother Wayne was doing *all day* for niggas turning state on him. She knew first-hand how we felt about snitches.

"Hey-Hey, Juice, how are you doing?" She stuttered in fear.

She know she foul. "I'm Gucci. Who you pregnant by?"

"Phatz." She hesitated then lowered her head.

"He in here?"

"No."

"Tell 'em to holla at me, ASAP. We needa link up about some money he owe somebody." I lied through my teeth.

"Okay, I will." She seemed happy that I wasn't trippin'.

"And tell yo brother to hit my line too." I walked off while the guilt soaked in.

I knew she knew exactly what I was getting at. I hoped my look of disgust appeared in her mind when she laid down at night. I never could understand that shit for the life of me. Bitches loved fucking with snitch niggas, then when they got pregnant by one, they cried like a bitch when real niggas send hot shit at both of 'em. Didn't they know they were a snitch nigga's main motivation to tell while he was sitting in a cold cell? Those rat muthafuckas used not wanting to leave their child and their girl as justification for flipping on their bros.

"I'ma start shootin' these snitch-loving bitches in their muthafuckin' heads, on Bloods." Gunna vowed as we peeled out the lot.

Marcellus Allen

Chapter 11
Juice

A few hours later I was sitting in the whip in the parking lot to Naughty's spot. I'd been posted up for ten minutes trying to get my mind right before I confronted my bitch. But the longer I waited the more madder I got for some reason. My bitch was on some sneaky shit and it hurt for me to accept it. *Dumb bitch.*

I stepped into the spot ready to slap the fuck out of her. Her perfume was the first thing to hit me after I walked in. I knew she was getting ready to hit the strip club, but I didn't give a fuck about none of that. I was on a mission. "Naughty! Where yo ass at!" I yelled in a Lean-laced voice. I'd been sippin' ever since we left the food truck. I was on one fo'real.

"I'm back here in the room."

I walked in and saw her getting dressed at the mirror like I expected. *The devil wears Prada.* I sat on the bed and stared a hole through her back. When we made eye contact and she saw the evil in them that's when she turned around looking concerned about me.

"What's wrong, baby?" She asked.

I pulled the pistol from my hoody then slowly placed it on the edge of the bed. "You. You thought I wasn't gon' find out, huh? You trying to line me up?" My eyes never left hers as I confronted her.

"What are you talking about, Davontae? Line you up?" She scrunched her face up while yelling in confusion. She was putting on a good show.

If I would've been tender dick I would've fell for it. But I wasn't. "Stay yo ass back. I don't trust you," I growled when she tried walking over to me. She stopped dead in her tracks. "Check these out real quick." I tossed my phone at her. I'd screen-shotted all of Jamar's pictures along with her likes and shit and saved them just for this moment. I stared through her while she scrolled through the flicks. I watched her face go from confusion to surprise in a few seconds.

She lowered the phone trying to look all sad and shit. "It's not what you're thinking, baby. I put that on my son." She vowed.

"Oh, yeah? Then why you ain't tell me he was out then?" I whispered, trying to contain my demons.

"'Cause last time I told you about him you got all mad and shit, talking about did I want you to throw the nigga a picnic." She made her voice deep trying to sound like me. "And you been keeping secrets from me too, nigga. Why you ain't tell me you was gon' kill Marcell? And I know Pete paid you for it too."

My hands were wrapped around her throat before she could finish her sentence. I'd hopped off the bed so fast and pinned her to that wall that I didn't even know I'd done it until it was done. Her smart-ass mouth had set me the fuck off. The fact that she tried to turn it around on me had forced me over the edge. That made me feel like she was really on some snake shit and was trying to cover it up. *Maybe Gunna was right.* Just the thought made me tighten my grip around her neck. "Stupid ass bitch. I should choke you out! You trying to set me up? You back fuckin' with that nigga?" I screamed in her face full of rage.

She kept trying to plead her case but she couldn't get any words out. Only sounds of her struggling for air could be heard. The more she tried to claw at my hands for her freedom the higher I lifted her in the air. When her eyes started rolling back in her head, I let her go. She collapsed to the ground, sucking in as much air as she could while coughing up a storm. I didn't feel no sympathy toward her though. I just didn't want her to die before I knew if Jamar was trying to line me up or not.

"You faggot ass bitch, you know I don't fuck with them niggas he in those pictures with! What kinda fuck shit you on? Huh?" I screamed.

"I'm sorry." She started sniffling in between her coughs. "I was gonna tell you."

"Is this nigga on some foul shit?"

She shook her head.

"How you know? You been all up under the nigga, haven't you?"

"I only seen him once since he's been out. He popped up at my mama's house to pick up Lil' Jamar, that's it. I haven't spent any

84

time with him."

I could see behind the fear in her eyes that she was telling the truth. "Naw, you just been spending time with the niggas pictures." I spat in a sarcastic tone. "You're a foul bitch, Naughty, and I'm done fuckin' with you. I can't trust you no more."

She lowered her head, unable to match my fiery gaze. I watched the tears roll down her face for a few seconds then I turned my back on her. I grabbed my duffle bag out of the closet then started transferring all the money from the safe into it. I heard her cry harder and harder with each stack that I dropped in the bag. I was a real street nigga to the core but hearing my bitch break down like that really fucked a nigga up.

I had to force my emotions to the side and rip my heart out my chest. I knew it wasn't no love out here in the streets. Love would only get you killed. But damn, I'd never expect no snake shit from her though. She'd kept it one-hunnid with a nigga from day one, and that's why the shit was really fuckin' with me. I kept my goon face on as I turned around. I snatched up my jewelry then made my way out the room.

Her words stopped me at the door. "On my father, I never spent no time with him, Davontae."

I stood there, soaking in her word. My pride was battling with the sincerity that I heard in her voice. I couldn't turn around to face her. I didn't wanna look into her eyes 'cause I knew they would suck me back in. "I don't trust you right now." I walked out even though everything inside of me told me not to. I just couldn't allow any signs of disloyalty to be around me, no matter the size of the infraction. My pride won.

* * *

Twenty-five minutes later I was parked in front of the corner store on 17th and Dekum. My anger had only gotten worse by the minute and I desperately needed to smoke somethin' before I ended up smokin' somebody. There was only one other car in the lot, but I didn't recognize it. In the hood we identified niggas by their cars, so anytime one drove past me my eyes were glued to it. They were like heat-seeking missiles, just ready to lock on to an enemy then destroy their whole existence.

But just 'cause I didn't recognize the white Impala didn't mean it wasn't a threat. I knew some grimy niggas who did shootings out of their sisters' cars. I peeped inside the store windows trying to get a good look at who was in there. I saw two niggas but couldn't get a read on their faces. *Fuck it.* I gripped the burner in my hoody then hopped out into the night. I hit the locks to the door 'cause my whole net worth was literally in the truck. All I had to my name was a lil' over fifty stacks and I'd be damned if it was stolen from me. A nigga was gon' have to catch a body if he wanted that bag. It would be a win-win for him if it came down to it. He'd come up on a nice lash and have a real killa's soul under his belt.

I shook the thoughts out of my head as I headed into the store. *I ain't dyin' until I avenge my brother's death.* Soon as I walked in, the dumb ass bell went off, betraying my silent entrance. A lil' short nigga appeared from behind the chips rack with his hand touching his waist. I recognized his face but couldn't place a name to it.

"What's brackin', Blood?" He hit me up on some Damu shit.

"What's up with it, gang?" I gave the nigga a lil' nod and kept walking. I didn't know him like that so there wasn't shit to talk about.

"Gang?" He said to my back. "Nigga, what gang?" He asked with too much bass in his voice for my gangsta.

I spun around like a tornado with my heat aimed at his chest through my hoody. "Murda Gang, nigga, what is it?" I closed the distance between us with two long strides.

"This Hit Squad on mine." He replied with some heart. But the look in his eyes didn't match his tone. He wasn't really ready to die about it. I had the drop on him and he knew it.

"And you said that to say what?" I shot back.

"Lil' Juice?" Jimmy called my name as he stepped from behind the same rack that his mans came from. "What y'all lil' niggas got poppin' off? We all family in here. Y'all take y'all hands away from them bangerz." He demanded like he was King Tut or somethin'.

I couldn't believe my luck. The nigga I'd been looking for, for weeks, was standing in front of me in the flesh. *Eat yo food.* My inner goon spoke to my gangsta. I turned my head slightly and saw the old man behind the counter staring at us. *I should body both these niggas then charge Pete double.*

"Juice, what's good?" Jimmy's voice snapped me out of my murder zone.

I noticed the lil' nigga had moved his hand away and they were waiting for me to. I put on a fake smile then took my hand out my hoody. The tension evaporated. "My bad, gang. Once a nigga get me in the goon zone it's hard for me to stand down without bloodshed." I locked eyes with Jimmy.

"You just like yo brotha, Blood." He complimented me then we shook hands.

"Yeah, I keep hearing that."

"This is my lil' homie Zane right here." He pointed to his mans. "Zane, this Lil' Juice right here. Big Juice was his brotha, the one that started the hood."

From the sparkle that glowed in his eyes I could tell that he'd heard about my brotha multiple times. "What's good, fam?" Zane stuck his hand out.

"What's good, gang?" I shook him up.

"Nigga, yo brotha a legand from the turf; you family to us. Anytime you run across somebody from the squad, just tell 'em who yo brotha is and they gon' lay the red carpet out for you." Jimmy said.

"Naw, I'm my own man out here in these streets just like everybody else. My brotha can't save me from the wolves from the graveyard. I'ma live and die on all ten toes though, I promise you that. But what's up with all the extra shit ya mans was on?"

He shrugged. "Some hating ass niggas killed Marcell so we on high alert right now. Ain't nobody moving without a shooter with them. Shit real right now."

"Yeah, I heard." I headed to the cashier to grab my Backwoods.

"We missed you at the funeral too." It was a questioning tone behind his statement. Or maybe it was my guilt. Either way I didn't like it.

"I don't really fuck with funerals like that," I shot back then paid for my Backwoods. "But we do needa start linking up on some family shit. We don't even got each other's lines." I sounded like I was hurt behind that fact.

We swapped numbers with promises to each other to link up in the near future. I definitely intended on keeping my word. My mood had dramatically changed from being heavy hearted behind my bitch, to feeling optimistic about my next kill. I was walking through the lot envisioning me putting a bullet in the nigga's head and me depositing twenty more stacks to my safe.

Loud music blasting from a car driving down the street brought me back to reality. It felt like time froze for a few seconds as the black Audi cruised down the block. I stared at it with my hand stuffed in my hoody and I could feel the heat coming my way from behind the tint. I kept muggin' that muthafucka until all I could see were taillights. I exhaled then loosened the grip on the smack.

Portland was real *jansky* like that and you just never knew when shit was gon' get real. Ever since the Crackerz pulled that gentrification stunt on us all, the hoods in North-East were fucked up. We all got packed up and shipped out like slaves to South-East Portland, better known as the 'Numbers' because of the high ass numbers on the street signs. So now North-East niggas run the numbers and try to still regulate their real hoods 20 to 30 away from where they lived. But all them dumb ass Crackerz did was make us more ruthless in the streets. Now we all lived amongst each other and we showed no mercy toward our opponents.

It wasn't no telling who was in that Audi and what they were doing out at midnight like that. I was in a historic Blood hood but that didn't mean nothing no more in North-East. *I gotta get home and put all this money and jewelry up.*

Soon as I made it to my door, I heard a few faint footsteps running behind me. I knew what it sounded like when somebody was trying to run and be quiet at the same time.

"What's up now, nigga!" A voice yelled from behind me.

I felt fear shoot through my veins as my heart skipped a beat. *I ain't dyin' like no bitch when a gun on me.* And just like that I drained that sucka shit out of my veins that had to been passed down genetically from my father's side and turned around to handle my business like a real nigga.

Boom! Boom! Boom! Boom! Boom! Bloc! Bloc! Bloc! We lit the night up from all the flames that were shooting from our barrels. It was two niggas with dreads standing in the street sending some hot shit my way. But I loved them type of odds. Two niggas couldn't guard Steph Curry so how the fuck did they think two rookies could stop a *real* shooter? I was more than determined to prove my theory to them. I kept moving through the lot, never stopping, exchanging shot for shot with them. *Boom! Boom! Boom! Bloc! Bloc! Bloc! Bloc! Bloc!*

"This what y'all niggas wanted?" I taunted them. My adrenaline was at the max level as I tried to knock a patch out of those niggas' dreads. Next thing I knew, my pistol was flying out of my hand and it felt like I got punched in my shoulder. *I'm hit.* I thought about running until I saw my banga laying a few feet away just calling my name. I wasn't dying from gunshots to the back.

"Aww, hell naw, Blood!" I heard from behind me.

Bloc! Bloc! Bloc! Boc! Boc! Boc! Boom! Boom! Boom! Shots went off from behind and in front of me as I scooped the gun up then started letting it bark.

"Hit Squad!" Zane yelled while he ran in front of me, letting his slugs fly.

Then Jimmy appeared next to me, letting his thang go off too. The two false assassins started backpaddling to their whip while still bustin' at us. They were all in when it was two on one but was scared of three on two. *Bitch ass niggas,* I thought while I was taggin' the paint off of their Audi as they fled the scene. We stood there in complete silence for a second, trying to gather our thoughts.

"I appreciate y'all niggas." I told them.

"I told you, you're family, Blood." Jimmy's words hit me harder than he could ever imagine. They fucked me up.

The sirens were blazing through the night and that was all the motivation we needed to haul ass. By the time I was bending the corner I could feel my arm on fire. It felt like a giant lighter was burning the shit out of me. I had to switch driving hands from the pain I was feeling.

"Bitch ass niggas tried to kill me?" I screamed then punched the steering wheel. "Ain't no preying on the predator, muthafuckaz." I growled in hate. Somebody had to die now.

Chapter 12
Naughty

"I don't know why you keep putting up with shit from that half-broke nigga anyways. Instead of putting his broke ass hands on you, he needa start touching some real money." Faith went off in my ear in her usual gold-digger fashion.

I needed some advice from my friend on how to get my nigga back, not on how to catch a millionaire. I should've known better. *I don't know why I called this bitch.* I questioned myself as I looked at my phone and rolled my eyes. I'd been sitting in the parking lot for twenty minutes listening to my best bitch go off about Juice. The shit wasn't helpful at all and all it did was stress me out even more. "Alright, bitch, it's time for me to get to work. I got bills to pay." I told her.

"Exactly. That's the problem. You're too beautiful to be paying some punk ass bills. Tell Juice to go get some real juice in the streets and go touch a fuckin' bag. Whatever, go shake your ass, trick."

I laughed at her dumb ass for the first time then hung up on her. I checked myself out in the mirror. I had to cover up the marks on my neck with a nice amount of make-up, but other than that I looked good as usual. I noticed my eyes were still a lil' puffy from all the crying I had done earlier. That nigga had me on the floor for over an hour pouring my soul out after he left. I had no intentions on going to work but decided that I needed to get my mind off the situation.

When I made it to the dressing room there was only one other chick inside. She was cool but I didn't really fuck with the bitches at my job like that. The strip clubs were cutthroat, and nobody was to be trusted, period. If I didn't fuck with the bitch before I was shaking my ass then I didn't fuck with her now. I gave her a 'what's up' nod as I made my way to my locker.

All I could think about was Juice while I peeled my clothes off. I knew I'd fucked up real bad and it was gon' take a whole lot of ass-kissing and work to get my nigga's trust back. But I'd forgiven his ass so many times for actually cheating on me that he'd have no choice but to forgive me. All I did was like a couple of pictures, I wasn't fuckin' the nigga. It wasn't like I didn't plan on telling Juice, I was just waiting on the right time to bring it up.

"Damn, bitch, why you so late?" Jessie came in being loud as usual.

She was standing there in a pink thong and bra with a stack of money in her hand. She was one of those bitches who actually liked stripping for a living. She did the shit every day with a smile on her face. One of her happiest days was when I came to her for help getting hired at the muthafuckin' club. But she was my girl and I definitely needed a shoulder to lean on. I just didn't wanna do it while we were both in a dressing room with our asses out.

"Nothing, I was just caught up in something. I'll tell you later." I tried to walk past her, but she grabbed my arm and looked in my face.

"Unn-unn, you've been crying and shit. What's the matter, mami?"

And just like that I started pouring my heart out to a half-naked bitch. It took ten minutes to tell her everything, then I started venting my frustration about stripping and all type of shit that'd been bothering me. "And I keep telling him that I don't wanna strip no more, but he keep slow-playing me. All he gotta do is hustle up the bread for my clothing line and I know it's gonna take off. He don't believe in me though." I spat my frustration.

"You gotta sit the nigga down and really express how you feel to him. Let him know your dreams and what you need from him. You know you gotta break shit down to these niggas like they're some grown ass kids."

I laughed at her while wiping away my tears. "But how am I supposed to get him back? I've been blowing his ass up and he won't answer."

She sucked her teeth. "That nigga ain't leaving you over no small shit like that. His pride just fuckin' with him right now, but he ain't going nowhere. He know it's a drought on real bitches right now."

She made me laugh again. "Bitch, you crazy. C'mon, we gotta

go get these niggas' money." I told her crazy ass.

By the time I got done fixing my make-up I was feeling way better and ready to make some money. I knew me and Juice's bond was way too strong to be broken over some shit like this. I was just gonna have to give him some time to come to his senses. I knew what I had to do.

I had been giving lap dances for over an hour when this white chick named Crissy came and got me from the bar. "There's this fine black dude with a lot of money asking for you in VIP." From the irritation I heard in her tone I could tell that he was only willing to spend his money on me. He probably had to pay her to deliver the message.

"Fine black dude? He's not one of my regulars?"

"Naw, I've never seen him before."

I made my way to the room trying to figure out who the hell could it be. I hoped it wasn't one of those tricks that wanted some ass or some shit like that. I hadn't tricked off with a client in years but that didn't stop them from asking. When Jamar first went to prison a bitch had to do whatever needed to be done to feed my son. But after me and Juice got serious, I fell back from that shit. He never judged me or threw it in my face either. He respected the fact that I was a go getta, period.

I had the faintest of hopes that it was Juice sitting on the couch. I knew he was way too prideful for that, but a bitch had to hope. All the hope went straight out the door as I sashayed my way in and got the surprise of a lifetime.

Sitting on the couch in all designers with a big ass smile on his stupid face was my baby daddy. "I brought you some money." He spread his arms then leaned back, taking my body in. All I had on was a G-string and bra that barley covered my big ass titties. His eyes were eating me up too.

"Jamar, why the fuck are you at my job? I don't find this shit funny at all." I threw my hands on my hips and gave him attitude. He was the source of my problems and that last nigga I needed in my face. *Juice would flip out!*

"I told you I brought you some money." He nodded at the stacks of money on the table. "Do you want it or not?"

"Not if you're on some fuck shit. You know I got a nigga." I spat.

He ran his hands through his face like he always did when he was trying to control his frustration. "Come sit down, Naughty, now." He demanded like he was the president or something.

I walked over and plopped down on the couch. "What, Jamar?" I rolled my eyes, snapped my neck, then stared him down.

"I don't pay for pussy and I damn sho ain't gon' pay my muthafuckin' baby mama for none. And you can stop throwing that nigga in my face too 'cause all that's gon' do is get 'em killed sooner than later. Now, I came to talk to you about what's on my mind."

"Sooner or later? What is that supposed to mean?" I hoped he wasn't planning on getting at Juice like that. I knew Jamar wasn't no pussy, but Juice was a-whole-nother animal. That nigga enjoyed killing people.

"Don't worry about all that right now, I got other shit on my mind." He had a devilish smile on his face now. "Can I get a dance first? Since I'm paying you all this money."

"Are you serious right now?"

"One dance." He responded.

"You giving me all this for one dance?" I knew there had to be a catch 'cause that shit ain't sound right.

"You right, I want two dances now. And I'm giving it to you 'cause it's my job to provide for you and my son." He claimed.

"Alright, two dances." I gave in against my better judgement. "And keep your hands to yourself too." I added while I stood up.

"Bitch, this gon' always be mine." He slapped me on the ass to show me who was in charge.

I wanted to flash on his ass but the Molly I'd taken before coming in had me feeling good now. When the DJ dropped my favorite Drake song, I started doing what I got paid to do. By the time the Migos came on, I was ass naked and grabbing my ankles, giving him the show of his life. After the song went off, he pulled me down in his lap and started trying to kick game. I listened for about five minutes then put my clothes back on. Everything he said sounded good, but I knew he just wanted a hole to stick his dick in.

"I hear you, baby daddy." I brushed him off while I collected the money off the table.

"I'm dead serious, Naughty. I'm ready to be the nigga that you need in your life. I'ma have enough bread to take care of y'all and you ain't never gotta strip again. We can start that clothing line you've always talked about too. Just say the word."

Oh, he really trying now. Nigga please. I turned around right before I walked out. I wanted to call his bluff for some reason. "Oh, is that right? Tell me the name of my clothing line then, since you're so sure of yourself," I challenged him.

He smirked at me then took a long swig of his Rosè. He was stalling.

"Just like I thought, a bunch of talking like always."

"Crowned by Her." He answered with an arrogant ass smirk that pissed me off.

"Whatever, nigga." I walked out on his cocky ass.

***

I woke up the next morning to my phone ringing like crazy. Every time it rung, I squeezed the pillow tighter over my head. *What this bitch want!* I didn't have the energy for her early morning gossip. Hearing that City Girls ringtone so many times was making me hate them bitches too. "What bitch?" I yelled in the phone. I knew all she wanted to do was get the tea about Jamar's ass. I figured Jessie filled her in on what had transpired in the VIP room. *Nosey bitch.*

"Bitch, don't be answering like that 'cause you over there sleeping off all types of pills and shit. Yo ratchet ass probably fell asleep with ya baby daddy's dick in yo mouth, trick." She flashed.

I knew it. "I know you ain't woke me up for that shit, you fuckin' thot." I slapped myself on the forehead mad, that I didn't turn the power off.

"Actually, I didn't. I woke you up to let you know that yo broke ass nigga got shot last night."

Her words made my heart drop to my stomach. "Don't play like that, Faith!" I yelled at her. I just knew she was playing with me. I'd just saw him hours ago.

"Bitch, I'm not playing! It's all on Facebook. The nigga all on there posting videos and shit thinking he Scarface."

I hung up on her ass and instantly got on his Facebook. My heart was skipping beats as I waited for his page to load up. Tears started rolling down my face non-stop, blurring my vision. I started reading his comments and instantly got mad. He was on there acting like he was untouchable, and everybody was on there feeding his stupid ass ego. After I watched his video, I was more than steaming. I hopped up, brushed my teeth, then shot up out of there.

I pulled up to his spot off of 15th Avenue twenty minutes later with a real attitude. *His ass is in there,* I thought as I parked right behind his truck. "He got me fucked up." I spat as I got out. I noticed two bullet holes in the side of his truck as I speed walked to his door.

His door flew open before I could pound on it. "What's good, sis?" Omar's big ass said while shielding me from walking in.

I mugged him not giving a fuck about the huge gun bulging from his waist. "I ain't trying to hear all that sis shit, Omar. Where is my nigga at?" I spat.

"He chilling right now. He don't trust you no more, sis. He don't wanna talk."

"He don't trust me no more?" *Oh, shit, I hope Jamar ain't the one shot at him.* I instantly felt the regret from giving Jamar those dances. I don't know what the hell I was thinking. "Either get out my way so I can fuck that nigga up, or I'ma take off on yo big ass right here on this porch and I'm not playing."

He didn't even flinch at my threat. But I wasn't playing with his big ass. My nigga had just got shot and I was gonna see him at any and all costs, period.

"Let her in, brody." I heard my nigga say. Just hearing his voice made my emotions get all stirred up. I was happy to hear that he was alive but was livid he hadn't called me.

Once Omar moved out of the way I bombarded Juice's ass. He was sitting on the couch with his shirt off and a Styrofoam cup in his hand that I knew had Lean in it. I saw an open wound on his shoulder that had a lot of dried up blood around it like he hadn't touched it since he got hit. He had some big ass gun laying on the table right in front of him like he was Tony Montana or something. The actual sight of him pissed me the fuck off.

"You got some nerve, muthafucka." I stood right in front of him with my hands on my hips, breathing fire. "You got time to make muthafuckin' home made videos and shit but not answer yo phone! Why I gotta hear from the streets about you almost getting killed? You know what that does to me? Huh?" I wiped away the tears from my face, hating the fact that I was looking weak.

"I find it real coincidental that right after I choked yo sneaky ass out I get shot at. I wonder did you call yo lil' boy-toy and he attempted to put his cape on?" He had the audacity to disrespect me like I was some type of foul bitch.

His words cut me so deep. It felt like he'd took a knife and cut out my heart piece by piece. I couldn't believe he would come at me like that. The tears started rolling nonstop. But then he smirked at me like I wasn't shit to him and that's when I lost it. I slapped the cup out of his hand, sending some of his Lean flying on him in the process. "You got me fucked up! Punk ass muthafucka!" I screamed my head off.

He looked at the syrup on his chest then back up at me. He found the shit amusing. "I ain't got time for yo basketball wives' antics, you dumb ass bitch. So, do us all a favor and go ahead and hit the Deion Sanders up out of here." He shooed me away like I was a muthafuckin' fly.

"Deion Sanders, huh?" I growled then bit my lip.

"Yeah, run up out of here."

Whap! I punched that nigga right in his jaw, rockin' his shit. I'd never attempted to put my hands on him before. I knew it was a fight I couldn't hope to win but it sho felt good. The look of surprise was all over his face as he held his jaw. I figured I might as well get in my licks before he whooped my ass. *Whap! Whap! Whap! Whap!* I got off where I was mad at. I was hitting that nigga with combos straight to the face. I wanted his punk ass to feel my pain. The whole time I was swinging I could hear Omar's fat ass cracking up with laughter. He must've really thought he was watching Jerry Springer or some shit. One minute I was connecting with Juice's jaw, then the next I was flying in the air.

He picked me up by the legs, held me in the air for a second then body slammed me on the couch. "Fuck wrong with you, bitch!" He shouted in my face, spit flying on me.

"Fuck you, muthafucka!" I started swinging and clawing at his face. I managed to get a good grip on his dreads, yanked him to me, then bit the shit out of his neck.

He didn't scream like a bitch like I expected him to, the crazy nigga roared like a fuckin' lion. Then he pulled away from me with ease and slapped the shit out of me. I saw a few stars. "Calm yo ass down before I really fuck you up." He spoke like we were having a regular conversation.

I was seeing red now. I coughed up a loogie with every intention to spit on him since he had my arms wrapped up.

Hearing the sound of spit made that nigga transform right in front of me. That look of pure evil appeared in his eyes that not even the devil himself could mimic. "If you disrespect me as a man like that, your life will end the moment you do it." He let my arms go then looked at the gun on the table before putting those demon eyes back on me.

I knew at that moment that he would really kill me. The crazed look he was giving me while straddling me forced me to believe he wasn't fully in control of his body. Not the nigga I fell in love with. I was witnessing the killer version of him. I did what any smart bitch with a sociopath in their face would've did. I swallowed my spit. When I did, the look of death evaporated.

"Get off of me, nigga. I hate you. I wanna go home!" I was more than ready to bounce. I felt like I'd gotten away with murder by socking him up and only getting slapped once. I'd definitely won that battle.

He got off of me then walked out of the front room without saying a word.

"You gotta give 'em some time, he'll come around." Omar said from the couch.

"Fuck that nigga!" I stormed out, really in my feelings. Shit hadn't gone like I'd expected it to go. I thought I was gon' cuss him out then we would have great make-up sex. Clearly, I'd thought wrong.

I peeled out his driveway with a river full of tears pouring down my face. For the first time since we'd been together, I really didn't know if we had a future together.

Marcellus Allen

Chapter 13
Juice

I popped a few Aspirin then stared at myself in the bathroom mirror. My bloodshot eyes reflected how tired I was and the blood I was about to spill. I smirked at myself like I was the Joker on some crazy shit. I found it funny that niggas actually thought they could hop out and fuck with the predator. I lived for shit like this— that gangsta shit. It made my dick hard. I couldn't wait to get the identity of those cowards so I could show 'em how it was done. They were going to be my food that I toyed with until my main dish came home.

I looked at my shoulder then got mad. *Never get disrespected without retaliation.* My brother's words rang loudly in my head. "Somebody gon' pay for spilling my blood." I vowed to the demon in the mirror. Not a drip of this real nigga blood was ever supposed to leave my body.

I touched the small knot on my forehead that Naughty put there and felt like whooping her ass. But I had business to tend to so I chopped it up for the time being. *Crazy bitch.*

Omar was posted on the couch smoking weed with a dumb ass look on his face. He found the shit funny. I snatched the Backwood from him. He started laughing. "Don't be mad at me 'cause you got yo ass beat by yo own bitch! How you get grazed and beat on in less than twenty-four hours. You hella weak, and ain't no murda gang shit." He kept on laughing.

I started laughing too. The shit was lowkey funny when I thought about it. "I should've beat her ass for taking off on me like that, on the gang." I hit the weed a few more times before passing it.

"You know damn well she ain't set you up, nigga."

"I know, I just felt like fuckin' with her for that sneaky shit she tried." I confessed. He nodded in agreement. As we stared into each other's eyes I saw that he had something on his mind. "What's on yo mind, nigga?" I asked.

"Naw, I was just thinking about the nigga Jimmy."

"What about him?" I already knew what was on his mind 'cause

101

the shit was heavy on mine too.

"He probably saved yo life and now you gotta kill 'em for some punk ass money. The shit just don't sit right with me." He spoke his mind.

I knew the triv was real when he spoke on it. Hearing Omar repeat what was already on my heart fucked me up. He was always the stone hearted one out of the crew. Most of Portland thought my nigga had no morals and wasn't loyal to nothing but himself. But they didn't know my nigga's heart. He wasn't loyal to nothing but the Gang, and I knew that for a fact. So, to hear him wanting to spare a soul made me really consider my conscience; the lil' I had left.

"I know, gang, but I already took some of the money and gave my word." I played devil's advocate. My phone starting ringing on the table, interrupting our conversation. My shit had been off the hook since the weak ass shooting went down. I was tired of talking about shit. I looked at the screen. *Blocked.* "Yo, who dis?" I answered on speakerphone then sat it down on the table.

"The nigga you've been looking for, Blood." I knew I knew the voice, but I couldn't place it.

Omar shrugged, not having a name either.

"I'm looking for a lot of niggas, so which one are you?"

"Nigga, this Phatz." He said his name like it was supposed to pump fear or something. Omar sat on the edge of his seat now.

I was surprised to hear from him and said the first thing to come to mind. "We gotta holla about some shit but not over the phone. When you wanna link up?"

"Oh, we gon' link up, sooner than you think too, nigga."

I looked at Omar to see if he caught the threat. He made a gun with his fingers letting me know what's up. I smirked.

"Nigga, you think I'm dumb or somethin'? I seen those muthafuckin' pictures you took with O-Dawg, nigga. I ain't forgot that you're his lil' lap dog."

His words had me hot as a muthafucka but I knew I had to play it cool in order to reel him in. Then I was gon' torture him for his disrespect. *Bitch nigga.* "That's what I needa holla at you about, nigga. O-Dawg want you to start kickin' him something off all the money you've been out here getting. What you did was foul, my nigga, so it's only right." I lied.

Him laughing in my ear had me gritting my teeth. "Nigga, if you don't knock it off. And I bet you he didn't tell you how he snitched on me first, did he? But fuck all that. I like you, lil' nigga, so I'ma spare you this one time. I'ma show you how dangerous I am, lil' nigga. I could've been killed you." Then the line went dead.

I couldn't believe his snitch ass had the heart to threaten me like I hadn't put mad niggas in the cemetery behind shit like that.

"I hate when snitch niggas still act like they wit' it." Omar spat in disgust.

"A lot of them still are wit' it." I shook my head at what had become of the streets. It felt like gangsta rats were runnin' the world and everybody accepted them. I lived by the old school creed: A rat anywhere was a threat to real niggas everywhere. "Just 'cause they told don't mean they won't bust their heat." I spoke the ghetto gospel to my nigga.

"Yeah, but they can no longer be considered real gangstas. Fuck them niggas, Blood."

"Yo, why his snitch ass try to put a jacket on my mans like that? Fuck nigga."

He sucked his teeth. "They always try that shit. That's they favorite excuse, and these pussies be going for it out here too. If you tell, you a snitch, period!"

"Don't worry about it. That nigga's a dead man walking—"

Boom! Boom! Boom! Boom! Boom! Boom! Boom!

"Get down!" I yelled then hit the ground as the bullets came flying through the house.

We both kissed the carpet and hoped we didn't get hit by a punk ass lucky bullet. I knew he was bustin' a choppa by how easy the bullets were ripping through the walls and destroying whatever they came in contact with. The sound was so loud I could barely hear myself think. I reached up and grabbed the AR-15 off the table. I thought about shooting back then changed my mind.

I aimed it at the door after all the dust and shells stopped flying. I prayed that he would try and walk through that door so I could feast on his snitch ass.

"You've been warned!" He shouted then I heard a door slam.

We both jumped up and ran outside but it was too late. I wasn't about to waste no shells on no fuckin' taillights.

"I'ma murder that nigga!" Omar vowed, wheezing and out of breath.

"C'mon, we gotta get all the guns and money up out of here before the boyz get here. Fuck!"

We broke back inside and started rushing, hoping to be gone before the bitch ass pigs showed up. *I'm kill this nigga.*

The next day we pulled up to Peninsula Park for the barbeque the Hit Squad were throwing for Marcell. I didn't give two fucks that I was the reason for the occasion or have a drop of sympathy. I planned on enjoying my ribs just like everybody else. We brought a few of our lil' homies with us just in case shit got ugly.

We mobbed inside the park fifteen deep, ready for whatever, but I didn't expect nothing to happen. Nobody outside of my circle knew I'd crushed Marcell and I knew Phatz snitch ass wouldn't show his face. The park was packed with his loved ones, hood rats and muthafuckaz who didn't even know him. But that's how it goes in the hood when a nigga dies.

"What's brackin' with y'all?" Breeze greeted us with a group of his Hit Squad homies.

The looks of retaliation was written on all of their faces. *Where was these looks at when my brotha died?* That shit had me hot. I got to envisioning putting holes through all of their soft ass chests.

"Shit, what's hood wit' y'all?" I replied as I shook him up.

He was my brotha's main nigga and the undisputed leader of his gang. I used to look up to him when I was a lil' nigga but soon as my nuts dropped I lost my respect for him. It wasn't 'cause he was pussy, 'cause he wasn't. He was known for bustin' his thang without any hesitation. My problem was he didn't kill the coward that smoked my brotha. One nigga died then he was content with that shit, but I was far from it.

Everybody shook each other up and when I locked hands with Jimmy, I didn't know how to feel. I'd accepted the contract on his life and killed his homie, and I knew there was no coming back from that. But he helped me keep the blood in my body and that shit touched my cold heart. *Ain't no loyalty in the jungle,* my demons reminded me. I was feeling like a soft ass nigga.

"I heard about the clack-outs you've been getting into, lil' bro. You know who it is?" Breeze asked like he really gave a fuck.

"Naw, but when I do, I'ma make an example out of him." I spat. I didn't want nobody to know about my beef with the rat. That shit disrespected my gangsta to the core.

"I've been thinking real hard." He put his hand over his chin like he was deep in thought. "Somebody killed Marcell out of the red, and now somebody's gunnin' for you. This shit gotta be connected. What you think?"

I think you're dumb as fuck. "I don't see how it could," was my response.

"A crab from Rose City Crips, who was also the nigga Freeze's relative, got killed a lil' while back. Know anything about it?" He smirked then stared through my eyes.

I shrugged. "I heard somethin' 'bout it."

"I think they're retaliating against us for it. It's only a few of them left but they had the element of surprise."

"Let's kill 'em then." Gunna agreed with his relative. He just wanted to kill some Crips like always.

We chopped it up for another ten minutes about the triv then went and grabbed some food. It turned out better than expected, way better. I had a group of niggas that I couldn't stand out hunting the heads of niggas that I hated. It also gave me easy access to Jimmy if I decided to pop his top. I was still indecisive about that body.

"I told you, you was wrong about that shit. These niggas really fuck wit' you." Gunna whispered in my ear while I ate my ribs.

I didn't give a fuck if they rocked with me or not, that was never my issue. I slung my own iron when it was do or die time. My problem was why did my brotha die in vain? I rubbed my palms together like Birdman did with a smirk on my face. "Fuck these niggas," was my response.

Marcellus Allen

Chapter 14
Juice

It took two weeks for us to get the drop on snitch ass Phatz but when I got the call, my whole spirit lit up. I was spending time with my daughter Ashley and her dolls when Mask served me the news. "You want me to sit on the spot for a few days till we come up with a plan?" Mask asked.

"Hell naw, we moving today. His snitchin' days are over. Let the homies know what time it is. Tell TJ to get the van and shit ready." I hung up with an evil smirk on my face.

"Oooh, daddy, you said a bad word!" My daughter pointed out.

"I'm sorry, baby." I kissed her then left the room. I found Brittney sitting on the bed putting her heels on, getting ready to leave. I was supposed to stay home and watch Ashley while she ran errands, but that shit went out the window. I had business to tend to. "Somethin' important just came up, baby, I gotta go handle it." I told her.

"You can't take her with you?" She asked.

"Naw, it's some street shit. I probably won't get back till after midnight." I gave her one of those faces.

She exhaled her frustration. "Fine, I'll figure it out, Davontae, have fun."

I pulled her into my arms. "Don't start that shit right now, baby. I've been giving you all my time for weeks now and you know it. Don't start acting stupid 'cause I gotta go handle some shit. I've barley left the house in weeks."

She knew I was spittin' the truth in her ear. After that rat took his anger out on my house, I moved in with her. I was never going to lay my head there again and I still didn't know how the fuck he knew I lived there. I'd been laying lowkey since the barbeque, gathering my thoughts and intelligence. I wanted niggas to think I was spooked and shook up, that way they'd poke their heads out. Plus, I kept hearing those Goonies niggas names being involved in that store shooting. I didn't know if it was them or Phatz but I planned on finding out.

"I know, I'm sorry, daddy. You got me all spoiled now since you moved in." She gave in.

I palmed her ass and tongued her down. "I'ma spoil you way more than you think. Just give me some time. Let me go handle my business. Don't wait up."

"Be safe, daddy, and I love you so much."

"Love you too, mama." I hit the switch on my soul and got in predator mode as I grabbed my heat and walked out the door. I didn't go kiss my daughter goodbye 'cause I didn't feel like explaining to her why I was standing her up. Plus, I didn't wanna see that look of innocence in her eyes while I was in killah mode. That shit always penetrated my gangsta and I didn't want that. I needed to be fully evil. I smiled at all the wicked shit I planned on doing to his snitch ass. "Ain't no muthafuckin' preying on the predator," I said as I started the truck up and peeled up.

It was a lil' after six o'clock and we'd been watching the food truck for hours. We were hoping that snitch ass Phatz would make a cameo, but he never did. I still couldn't believe that he had the balls to move his truck like I wasn't gon' find the shit. He moved it out of North-East to the Numbers in hopes that it would blend in with the other twenty or so out there. But we found it off of 102nd Street with ease and we had no plans of losing it again.

"Blood, his snitch ass ain't coming here. So, either we hop out and crush his rat-loving bitch or we go and kidnap her ass. I'm tired of this waiting shit, on the gang." Gunna spat his frustration.

We'd been sitting in the van six deep for hours and everybody had complained at least once. I stared out the rain-smothered window debating on how I wanted to handle the triv. There wasn't no customers in sight and the rain was pouring down real hard, discouraging any future clients.

"I say we just go and smash that bitch and make him look for us." Flash spoke up.

"Killing her ain't gon' get us closer to the plug, that's pointless. Plus, I told y'all we ain't killing her on behalf of Wayne." I responded.

"Let's go get her then." TJ spoke in a low tone like always. He sounded bored with the whole situation.

"Mask, you and TJ follow me." I looked over at Gunna. "Be ready to pull off. I'ma go get her."

"'Bout time, nigga!"

I didn't even respond to his ass, I slid on my mask instead. I didn't need no good Samaritans trying to remember my face or taking no fuckin' pictures. White people in Portland were known for shit like that. After my niggas were masked down we hopped out into the rain and speed-walked across the street. All the other stores were closed so the lot was empty and fortunately for us the truck faced the other way. So, we were able to get up on it without her seeing us.

We stood by the door for a second pulling our pistols out and listening for any sounds. The last thing we wanted to do was snatch her up while she was on the phone. Especially with Phatz snitch ass. He'd probably call the FBI or some shit like that. I pointed at Mask to open the door after I didn't hear no talking. Soon as he yanked it open, I rushed in with the steel pointed right at her stomach. I knew that would cause instant cooperation.

"Aahhh!" She screamed with her hands covering her belly like that could stop some bullets.

"Yell again and I'ma crush you, Anna."

Her eyes lit up at the sound of her name. The fear was all over her face while her body was trembling. "The money is over there." She pointed to a cash register.

I almost slapped her dumb ass for disrespecting my gangsta. "Sit down. We needa talk, Anna." I pointed to the chair with my heat. She sat down, looking like she was ready to give birth out of fear. I pulled my mask off, violating the code of the wicked. I wanted her to see my face. See the sincerity in my eyes. I shook my dreads away from my face so she could see the full picture. I watched her eyes grow wider as she recognized me. She knew what time it was. "You already know what the triv is, Anna, don't you?" She nodded while the tears started falling from her eyes. "We not gon' kill you on behalf of yo brotha, but you gon' take us to y'all spot so we can kill Phatz; understand?"

"Yeah." She started sniffling and crying harder. "I understand." I saw nothing but pain and sadness in those pretty eyes of hers. She knew what I was about. She knew her life was about to be dramatically altered forever. She had to choose between her and her unborn, or her rat ass boyfriend. She chose wisely.

"My niggas gon' drive yo whip and you gon' get in the van with me. If you scream or try any dumb shit, I'ma shoot you in yo stomach and let you bleed out in the street; understand?"

"Yes." She answered.

I made her give up the address and car keys then we were on our way. I wrapped my arm around her waist while we crossed the street. It looked like I was just helping my pregnant wife if any good Samaritans were looking. I had to keep my mask off to complete the act. I repeated my earlier threat in her ear while we walked. But it was pointless. She already knew my get down and she didn't wanna play with it. The door slid open and I looked around to see if anybody was watching. The coast was clear.

"Why the fuck you take your mask off?" Gunna asked after we made it off the block.

"Go to Seventy-Ninth and Flavel; that's where they live." I didn't feel like discussing no irrelevant shit with the nigga.

"Is he there right now?" Omar growled. He couldn't wait to wrap his hands around that rat for sending those bullets through the house.

"I'ma find out right now." I passed Anna her phone back. "Make the call, and don't forget it's his life or y'alls." I pointed the heat at her stomach.

She nodded. "Okay."

"Wipe those tears and get yourself together. Street niggas can hear tears and detect stress over the phone. If you fuck it up, my niggas not gon' hesitate to crush you." I gave her the real.

It took her a few minutes to get it right. I kept my eyes locked on hers the whole time. She stared into mine intensely before she placed the call. Her eyes begged my soul for mercy. I nodded in agreement.

"What's good, baby?" The snitch answered.

My heart sped up from hearing his voice. I wanted him dead in the worse way. I looked at Omar. I could feel the heat coming from behind his mask. The tension could be felt all through the van.

"Umm, nothing. I just left the truck, headed to the house. Are you home?"

"Naw, but I'll be there in an hour or two." He confirmed.

"Okay, I'll see you later then."

"A'ight, baby, love you."

"Love you too."

She started crying again soon as she hung up. But it wasn't gon' change nothing. Her tears were falling on deaf ears and cold hearts. Plus, she didn't really love that nigga, she just thought she did. 'Cause if she did, she would've died for him. You were supposed to give up your life for your loved ones, not agree to set 'em up to save yourself. But I couldn't blame her for not wanting to die for a snitch, I wouldn't either.

"This the one right here?" I asked her twenty minutes later when we pulled up to the house.

"Yes." She replied.

I stared at the two-story crib with hate then looked around the neighborhood for any sign of life. There wasn't a soul in sight which made our job that much easier. It looked like one of those nice ass neighborhoods where everybody minded their own business. I felt the envy rushing through my veins.

"Snitch nigga living better than us. Fuck they do that at?" Gunna spat like he was reading my mind.

"Do you usually park in the driveway or what? And don't try to lie, we know all the tricks there is." I warned her.

"I always park in the garage." From the confused look on her face I knew Phatz hadn't laced her with an emergency plan.

"A'ight, I'ma take her in. Y'all park the whip down the street. I'ma unlock the front door for y'all." I stepped out into the night then helped Anna out of the van. The rain had stopped pouring but the ground was still wet, and the air smelled like rain. I kept my mask off while I walked over to her car. The last thing we needed was some nosey ass Cracker to see me jumping out of a van with a mask on with a pregnant bitch.

"A'ight, gang."

I pulled Anna close to me while we walked up the driveway. If anybody popped out of the garage shooting I was gonna put one in her temple. I didn't expect nothing to happen, but one thing the streets had forced me to learn was to always be ready for the unexpected. But nothing happened, and five minutes later I was opening the door for Gunna and Flash.

"Everything Gucci?" Gunna asked after they sat down on the couch. I noticed they took their masks off in the van.

"Yeah, we good, just gotta wait on this pussy." I answered.

"It look like they living real good to me." Flash stood up looking around.

"Yeah, he got a nice sized safe in their bedroom too. She claim she don't know the combo either."

"He'll give it up, one way or another." The smirk on his face displayed his ill intentions.

After an hour of waiting, I ended up falling asleep on the couch like it was my shit. All the Lean sippin' and pill poppin' I'd been doing was starting to take a toll on my body.

"Get up, he here." Omar shook my leg.

I bounced up with my heat in my palm on some real-life Jason Bourne type of shit. I was dyin' to split the nigga's wig. Everybody was standing around in the dark except for TJ. All of our eyes were locked on Gunna as he peeped from behind the blinds. Then the silence was shattered by the garage door being opened. My heart skipped a beat. We all looked at each other for a split second then rushed to the kitchen. We'd been over the plan a dozen times, there wasn't shit to be said.

I sat on the counter with my pistol resting on my lap. I wanted my face to be the first thing his snitch ass saw when he walked in. The rest of the gang surrounded the door so they could snatch him up soon as he stepped in. The garage closed then we heard his car door open and shut. My adrenaline was at an all-time high.

"One up top, Ahky. Somethin' stocky in the choppy." He opened the door rapping Mozzy like he was really 'bout dat life.

Once he hit the lights and saw my demonic face staring at his, all the bitch came out of him. Fear instantly appeared in his eyes. His hands fumbled with his waist then Omar smacked him across the head with his Desert Eagle. He grunted then dropped to his hands and knees. Soon as he did, my niggas started stomping him out like the pussy he was.

"Fuck you rappin' Mozzy for, nigga! Rap that Takashi 69 snitch shit!" Gunna shouted while putting his Nikes to his face.

They whooped his ass some more and took his pistol until he was laid out and no longer trying to fight back. I just stared and shook my head at a nigga who's gangsta I used to really respect. *Is this how it ends?* I didn't understand how a nigga could go from being a top-shelf gangsta, to getting stomped out in his own kitchen for being a rat. I guess Jay-Z said it the best, *It was all good just a week ago.*

"C'mon, let's take 'em upstairs." I hopped off the counter far from satisfied with the beating he'd received. I stared at him with pure hate as they lifted him up from the floor. His nose was leaking, his lip was busted and from the looks of his eye it would be swollen the next day. But having a black eye the next morning would be a miracle beyond imagination for him. Lucifer was calling for his soul and I was hell bent on delivering it to him.

"I should've killed yo bitch ass when I had the chance, pussy." Phatz spat a blob of spit right next to my feet.

"If that snitch ass blood would've touched these real nigga shoes I would've slit yo baby mama's throat right in front of you." I spat.

"Fuck you and that bitch, Blood, she set me up." He shot back to my surprise.

"Ya better keep Bloods out ya mouth, you fuckin' snitch." Flash checked him.

"Hurry up and get this rat upstairs so we can tape his mouth shut. I'm tired of hearing him talk." I said

It took us a few minutes to drag him up the stairs. He'd decided to try and fight us like that was gon' make a difference. Mask got tired of the dumb shit and started pistol-whipping 'em, forcing him to get some act right.

"Here go the nigga you love." I told Anna as we drug him into the room.

We had her tied up with her mouth taped so she couldn't say shit. But that didn't stop her from trying to talk through the duct tape.

"Look what you did, you stupid ass bitch." Phatz spat venom in her direction.

We taped his hands and feet together without much of a fight. He was tired of getting his ass beat. He was staring daggers at his bitch and all she could do was put her face down and cry. He would've killed her himself if we would've let him. I could feel the hate seeping out of his pours.

"What's the combo to the safe?" I asked as I pulled my phone out.

"Fuck y'all niggas, I ain't telling y'all shit!" He got his gangsta back.

"If you don't, I'ma cut yo bitch stomach open and let you see yo son before you die."

He didn't flinch, blink or even breath hard at the sound of my threat. He truly didn't care. "Fuck that bitch, she signed her own death warrant. I ain't about to let her live so she can go suck the next nigga's dick." I was expecting to hear him say that.

Anna started crying even harder. I'd already told her we wasn't gonna kill her so she must've really been hurt by what he was saying.

"This is what happens when you fuck with a snitch nigga. They ain't got no morals or loyalty to nobody. A fuckin' rat will eat it's on mother in order to survive," I gave her some game to remember. I looked at Phatz while my phone was going off. "It's time for you to answer for yo ghetto sins." I smiled for the first time.

"What's Mobbin', nigga?" O-Dawg's face appeared on the screen.

"I got a surprise for you." I told him

"Blood, it better be good. I had this bad bitch bustin' it open for a real nigga when you texted me. Shit, my dick still hard."

I didn't even wanna respond to that shit. I had something better than words could ever explain. First, I put the camera on Gunna though. I wanted to make him anticipate his surprise.

"Sup, bBood? We out here holding it down for you on the gang." Gunna got all excited.

"What's brackin'? What's the triv?" O-Dawg was ready to get to the point.

I spun the phone around to Mask next, then let him see the rest of the hittaz. They all hit 'em up with the gang with smiles on their faces. We were all amped up to see our real nigga doing good behind those walls. My nigga was a real life living legend.

"I got yo favorite lil' homie with us too." I put the phone right in Phatz's face.

They stared at each other with hate, not saying nothing for a full minute. I could literally feel my nigga's hatred through the phone. Phatz snitch ass had the audacity to stare him down like he was a real killah getting ready to meet his maker.

Whap! I backhanded his snitchin' ass. "That's for bustin' at me outside the store, pussy." I spat.

He spat the blood out and smiled. "If that was me then you would've died that night, lil' nigga." The look of fire in his eyes told me he was telling the truth. *Who the fuck shot at me?*

"How the fuck you gon' snitch on the nigga that created you? I would've took a bullet for you and this how you do me? I'ma die in this muthafuckin' cell, Blood!" I could hear and feel the pain through his hateful words. We were listening to a man with a broken heart.

"He told me and Juice that he told 'cause you snitched first." Omar blurted out.

"Say what!" He yelled. I shook my head at Omar. "You out there falsifying my name?"

"Nigga, you a bitch! If it wasn't for us putting in all that work for you, you wouldn't get half the recognition that you do. I'ma kill you in hell, pussy!"

"This new wave of snitches are hard as a muthafucka, huh? That's a'ight 'cause you gon' die a bitch ass rat. Y'all can kill this rat, I'm done talkin'." O-Dawg spat.

Gunna gave me the nod. He wanted me to negotiate our new terms with O-Dawg before we killed Phatz. I shook my head. "How you want 'em done?" I asked instead.

"Put 'em on his knees so he can die like the coward he is."

Smack! Omar dropped him out of the chair then they held him up on his knees. I passed the phone to Mask so O-Dawg could watch me work. Phatz stared right into the phone with no fear. He was ready to die.

"You should've been this tough in the interrogation room, pussy." I spat as I placed the heat to his dome.

Boom! Blood splattered everywhere while his body slumped forward. *Boom!* I put one more in his back 'cause snitches didn't have no spine. The whole time Anna was crying and screaming behind the duct tape. She was wasting her energy though. The rat was dead.

"Yo, who that y'all got tied up back there?" O-Dawg asked.

"His pregnant baby mama. We had to use her to get in."

"So, why she ain't dead yet?"

"'Cause she pregnant and she's Wayne's lil' sister. Wayne that's from Bloodhounds. I don't wanna do him dirty like that." I explained to him.

"Well, she gon' do y'all dirty like that. She gon' snitch as soon as the cops get there. Don't make the same mistakes I made. Think about Olay, lil' nigga."

"The boys gon' be on us about her being pregnant though. We gon' be hot." I tried to reason with him. But thinking about Olay did fuck me up. Nobody seen that shit coming.

"Shit gon' get hot, no doubt. But if she lives y'all gon' be more than hot, y'all gon' get cooked. So, look in yo niggas' eyes and decide if you're willing to put them in a cell for life 'cause you decided to let a bitch live. She ain't innocent, she chose to live a life of a rat when she laid down with the nigga. I know her brotha taught her better than that. I chose you for a reason. Don't make me lose respect for yo gangsta." The screen went black.

I looked at each one of my brothas in their eyes then sat down on the bed with my hands on my head. I didn't wanna betray Wayne, a nigga that used to give me money after Juice died. I damn sho didn't believe in catching innocent bodies. That was for suckaz. I looked Anna in her eyes. She was scared, she was crying, she knew her fate was in my hands.

"If we lose his respect then we lose the chance to get the connect." Gunna said then stood next to her with his heat aimed at her temple.

She started crying harder and shaking her head. I could clearly hear her screaming *please*. Our eyes never left each other's and she was pleading with my soul for mercy. I was gonna turn my head but realized that wouldn't be respected by the gangstas in the afterlife.

So, I buried my conscience. With my eyes still locked on hers I spoke to Gunna. "Kill her."

Boom! The single gunshot blew half her face off, silencing her forever. Her lifeless eyes stared into my cold ones, no longer begging for mercy. If anything, they were asking me why.

"If you run with rats then you eat the cheese too." Mask reminded the room of the code we lived and die with.

"Facts." I stood up with a new purpose in life. I was gonna get rich or get killed for tryin'. All my life I just wanted to murder the man that killed my brotha. Now I wanted every single dollar and every drop of power that came with this shit. Having her killed in order to secure our connect really did something to me. Giving the order to kill an unborn child had stained my soul forever. If there really was a hell then I was going straight there. "Two more rats to smash then we chasing millions." I kicked Phatz for disrespecting the game before I walked out. I came in a beast but walked out the house a monster on the loose. I was about to fuck the whole city up.

Marcellus Allen

Chapter 15
Juice

I laid low in the house for the past three days while the police turned the heat up. Every time I answered the phone or checked Facebook somebody new had just got harassed by Gang Task over that triple homicide. I knew the snitches were out working like a muthafucka trying to do the pigs jobs for them but we were in the clear. Nobody had our handles in their mouths and that was a blessing from the game gods in itself. But if muthafuckaz thought shit was about to die down then they were sadly mistaken. We were just getting started. We had lines on Olay and Ralo and planned on killing them both in the near future. Plus, my pride and my gangsta were pleading for revenge on whoever tried to end me at the corner store. Niggas was gon' feel it about that one.

"You think we gon' have to crush this nigga?" Omar asked as we pulled into the Chipotle parking lot.

After giving it much thought I finally decided to spare Jimmy's life. The real nigga in me just couldn't kill him after he helped me keep my blood in my body. I hoped Pistol Pete would overstand where I was coming from and wouldn't try to hold me to my word. I hated to break my word, but I couldn't take the man's life for no money. It would never sit right with me. I exhaled deeply. "I don't know, brody, but either way I'm not changing my mind. It ain't like he paid me upfront for both bodies. So, he can use that other twenty bands to pay somebody else to do it." I checked the clip to my Mac 11 as I looked around the lot.

"Well, that's what it is then, nigga."

"C'mon, let's get this shit over with."

I hopped out and looked around the crowded shopping center lot and hoped we didn't have to shoot it out in broad daylight 'cause we would fa'sho be going to jail. *I don't know why the fuck he wanna meet up in a crowded place anyways.* Soon as we walked in, we spotted Pistol Pete, and his homie Chris started walking toward us.

"Grab us some food while I holla at this nigga." I told Omar then walked off.

Me and Chris nodded at each other in passing. I could feel his energy and I wasn't feeling the shit. I knew it was a reflection of Pete's attitude toward me. I wasn't worried though, I had a clip full of hot shit that changed attitudes and lives forever for fuckin' with me.

"What's good with it?" I shook him up then sat down.

He was sitting there with all his jewelry on and trying to look tough like he was some type of Mafia Don. I wanted to snatch his diamonds off then laugh in his face.

"Shit, Cuz, you tell me. What's crackin'?" He spat like he was really 'bout it.

"In regards to what?" I fucked with him.

I watched the frustration run across his face. "I paid you to do a job and it's only half done. I'm starting to feel like you're playing with me, Cuz."

"Naw, I just decided I can't do it."

"Say what?" He screwed his face up.

I explained the story to him of how Jimmy helped me defend my life and how that changed my mind. But I made it real clear to him that I wouldn't tell Jimmy about the hit or warn him of any future ones. I just couldn't be the one to do it.

"I paid you to do a job, period. Hitmen ain't supposed to have feelings and shit." He spat after hearing what I had to say.

"You gave me twenty upfront, right? That twenty was for Marcell, so just keep the other twenty and we're good. Neither one of us loses shit. No harm, no foul." I replied.

"If you void a contract then it's fully void, not halfway. That means either give me all the money back or finish yo breakfast."

We stared at each other with a newly found hate for each other. Neither one of us blinked. I did my best to hold my anger in check, but he was really testing me. I stood up to leave before I made the news. "I've said all I came to say." I spat.

"You might wanna stop feeling so untouchable. Even killers get money put on their heads." He threatened.

"Just like bitch niggas with money get killed every day in the streets. I'ma give you a few days to get yo mind right before I have to spill it on the pavement." I gave him the look of death then walked away before I caught a life sentence.

"What's good? Is it going up?" Omar whispered at the door while he mugged Pete.

"We gon' kill 'em later, gang." I spoke through clenched teeth.

I speed walked to my truck. The whole time I was talking myself out of shooting that muthafucka up. My anger was ready to spill out.

"I'm telling you right now, gang. I'ma shoot that bitch ass nigga in his muthafuckin' head." I punched the steering wheel. "This nigga was talkin' like he was Big Meech or somethin'."

"What? What his bitch ass say?" Omar was ready to ride like usual. I stopped the truck right in front of Chipotle.

"Give 'em his twenty bands back or kill Jimmy, no negotiating. Then, the pussy said even killaz can get a bag on his head. It's guns up."

Omar stared at them niggas through the window for seconds without saying nothing. His big ass was in bodyguard mode now. "Well let's go up then." He turned and looked at me dead in the eyes. He was ready to take it there.

"It's too much money on the line." I calmed my gangsta down and drove off.

We drove for five minutes without speaking a word out loud. We were stuck in our own thoughts.

"I think I know who shot at me." I said out of nowhere.

"Who you think it was?"

"The Goonies. They're the only ones that makes sense to me. I think they're too caught up with them Gas team niggas to just come all the way out with the beef. If they can catch me lowkey, they'll do it. If not, then they gon' wait till all their other funk is over with." I explained.

"Let's pull up on their block and see what's up then." He made it sound so easy.

"A'ight, fuck it then." I gave in after much thought.

The Goonies stronghold was in the Ville, a historic apartment complex in North Portland. It was a goldmine that niggas stayed killing over. O-Dawg used to control them but now all different cliques were fighting for control.

"Yo, why you say it was too much money on the line back there?" Omar asked ten minutes later.

"Oh shit!" I slapped myself on the head. "I forgot to tell y'all I hollered at O-Dawg last night about the plug and he's with it. It took a lot of convincing but he eventually agreed to our terms. We're about to be on." I smiled for the first time.

"We need to hurry up and kill them rats."

"Facts."

When we finally pulled into the Ville, it was muthafuckaz every where. Old people, kids, and everything in between. I drove slow looking around until I recognized a face.

"Yo Chelsey, where Ace and them at?" I asked this chick I knew with a smile on my face.

"What's up, Juice? Him and Flocko are on the basketball court with everybody else." She gave it up.

"Yup, good lookin'."

"When you gon' call me?"

"Soon, I'm late for our meeting." I drove off before she could stick her head in my whip. That bitch stayed burning niggas and I wasn't about to be next. Fuck that!

I drove around the complex until the courts came into view. When they did, we immediately saw who we were looking for. It was Ace, Flocko and four other niggas standing in the middle of the court like they owned the world. It was a group of hood rats posted across the street being loud trying to get their attention. *Bitch ass niggas.*

"What we doing, gang?" Omar asked.

I focused on two of the niggas that had long dreads and felt it in my soul that they were the shooters. I never saw their faces that night but their body types were the same and I felt it. "The niggas with the dreads shot at me," was my response.

"What we doing, gang?" He repeated, letting me know he was with whatever.

"How many shots you got?"

122

"Seventeen, all hollow tips."

I had thirty in the Mac and was ready to use every single one of them. My anger was rising again. I parked the whip right in front of the groupies.

"Let's check their temperatures." I said, then hopped out.

"Damn, that's yo Escalade?" One of the chicks asked. I was focused on the task at hand so I didn't even look in their direction.

The Goonies had their eyes locked on us by the time we were halfway in the street. All of their hands shot to their waists but that didn't deter me from my mission.

"Y'all niggas lost or somethin'?" Their bitch ass leader Ace asked.

"Naw, we were rockin' with some bitches and saw y'all and decided to see what's up." I got right in their space.

"See what's up with what?" Ace shot back with hostility.

"These rumors I've been hearing a lot of recently." I looked at both of the lil' niggas with the dreads. They had flames bouncing around in their eyes. They were ready to go. "I keep hearing y'all want me dead for some reason. Then, I get shot at and y'all's names keep poppin' up."

"Rumors are rumors but speaking of them. We keep hearing that you're the one who killed Lil' Shawn for O-Dawg. What's up with that?"

I smirked. "Rumors are rumors."

"Aye nigga, you might wanna remember where the fuck you at." Flocko jumped in.

I saw him and his niggas tense up. I eased my hand toward the Mac.

"I know where I'm at, nigga. This the spot y'all was scared to even look at when the Mob niggas were out here. Niggas weren't asking questions about Lil' Shawn back then."

Everybody yanked their guns out as soon as I finished my sentence. I guess I touched on a sore spot.

"Nigga keep talkin' and y'all won't make it out of the North." Ace was hot now.

"Today is a good day to die. The sun is out, the birds are

chirpin'." Omar spoke up ready to let his Desert Eagle go off.

"Fuck the North, nigga." I spat a loogie on the ground to enforce my point. "And don't think that I don't know that these two suckaz are the ones who shot at me. If it weren't so many people out here, I'd let this Mac chew y'all the fuck up!" I was turnt up.

Ace smirked at me. "I can't wait to kill y'all weak ass North-East niggas. Get the fuck up out of here before I forget how much money we're making out here."

"These niggas are out here trippin'. Welcome to the life! Ville life!" A female voice came from behind me.

I looked and saw that the hood rats had us going live on social media. It was time to bounce.

"I'ma see y'all niggas." We started walking backwards with our hands still gripping the heat we had.

"Say less, nigga."

We hopped in and drove off without anybody letting any shots off. I was so mad that my hands were trembling on the steering wheel.

"Niggas are really hard today, huh?" I asked while still navigating through the complex.

"Naw, we acting like bitches today, on the gang. This ain't no murda Gang shit, Blood." Omar spat.

His words hit me hard as a muthafucka. It wasn't like me not to crush a nigga right there on the spot. I stopped the truck in the middle of the street.

"What you wanna do, nigga?"

"Turn this bitch around and I'ma show you. I don't give a fuck about them cellphones, them bitches, none of that!" He meant every word too.

I stared in his demon possessed eyes for a few seconds then busted a U-turn. Now my own nigga had me fucked up! I wasn't gon' speak on it though. I had thirty friends to do that to me. I parked around the corner from our original spot.

"Don't come back with nothing left either." I demanded then hopped out with the engine still running.

I let the Mac hang by my leg while I speed walked down the

street. I heard somebody yell gun from across the street but I didn't give a fuck. I was on a mission and had my eyes focused ahead of me. I bent the corner and saw those pussies still standing there, probably talking about me. *I got somethin' for y'all to talk about.* I started walking faster, trying to get close as I could before they could spot me. Then, those hood rats saw us and started screaming.

"MurdaGang!" I yelled so it wouldn't be no mistaking who did it. Then, we let loose.

Blatt! Blatt! Blatt! Blatt! Boom! Boom! Boom! Boom! Boom!

One of the cowards with the dreads folded up and dropped instantly. I knew he wished he would've killed me at the store. Me and Omar stood side by side, airing those niggas out like we were trained to do. I saw him out of my peripheral holding his heat with both hands like the police did. That's what niggas did when they were really trying to knock a specific enemy's head off. I was waving my shit at all them pussies. I hated them all equally.

Blatt! Blatt! Boom! Boom! Boc! Boc! Boc! Boca! Boca!

They let their nuts drop and started bustin' back at us. We were having a full fledge shootout and I wouldn't want it any other way. My adrenaline was at the max as I zig zagged in the street, dodging bullets. Glass shattered from the car I was standing next to. I didn't feel no fear. That shit pumped me up.

"Come get it like Shawn did!" I taunted.

"You gon' die for that!" Flocko yelled back as he grabbed one of the hood rats for a shield.

She screamed her head off.

My Mac didn't discriminate though. I aimed at both of them.

"I'm getting low!" Omar told me.

We started backpedaling toward the truck while still letting the slugs fly. The pussy nigga with the dreads was still laid out like the bitch he was. The other nigga with the dreads stood over him while firing at me. I respected any killa that would stand over their fallen comrade and let that thang bust for their protection. Most niggas wouldn't do that. But respect or not, I was trying my best to leave 'em laying there next to his mans. I lost the lil' respect I did have for them other pussies, though. They hid behind cars while they shot at us the whole time. We were in their hood! Standing in the street like we had a death wish or something. And they were ducking their heads like a fuckin' ostrich.

"MurdaGang!" I let 'em know one more time before I jumped behind the wheel.

I didn't start breathing regular until we made it out of the Ville without a scratch on us. There wasn't a feeling on this earth like clackin' it out in broad daylight and getting away with it. The rush was real.

"My shit empty nigga, what about yours?" Omar held his pistol in the air with a grin on his face.

I had shells left and he knew it. "If I didn't have to save yo weak ass, I would still be back there shooting." I responded.

"Nigga I was on shit, on the gang. And that nigga with the dreads was on yo' line too!"

"That's 'cause I dropped his man's right in front on him. And don't be trying to take credit for my score either, nigga. I know how you and Gunna like doing that shit."

We were talkin' shit all the way to his spot. It helped us keep our minds off the actual bullshit. Being nervous and over-anxious to get home after a shooting could be the downfall of a perfect drill. I knew jailhouses full of niggas that got away at the scene but got blurped before they could make it home. One false move in front of a cop car could cost you your freedom. Especially, when the pigs were already looking for you. Shit was real in the streets.

But we made it back like all real niggas were supposed to. After I dropped brody off, I slid back to Brittney's. I'd been staying there since that dead snitch shot my spot up. I cracked a smile at the thought of his upcoming funeral. *Snitch nigga.* Then, my thoughts drifted to the conversation I'd had earlier with O-Dawg.

"So, you're telling me that y'all wanna be dope boyz now?" He wanted clarification.

"We been selling work our whole lives. Might as well take it to another level. We need a consistent way of eating. You gon' fuck with us or what?"

He laughed in my ear. "I wanna know how y'all niggas are

gonna convince muthafuckaz to cop from y'all."

"Ain't none of them other cliques having problems, especially The Goonies. They been shooting the town up just like we have. Matter of fact, fuck all that. We gon' kill every other Major dealer if we got to. The clientele gon' be there." I spat.

"So, you gon' take care of all that triv for me in exchange for the plug, huh?"

"Yeah, introduce us and front us the reup money." I made it clear.

After a long silence, he said the words I needed to hear. "Handle that triv and I'll make the intro. We'll sort the details out later."

When I got to the spot, both Brittney and my daughter were gone. I needed the silence anyway. I sat on the couch and planned our takeover. I wasn't gon' take no prisoners either. One slip in the jungle would cost a real nigga his life. The first time a nigga or bitch played with' me, it was gon' be off with their heads. I was gon' get rich or get killed for trying. I was done living in apartments and shit. I knew too many soft hearted muthafuckaz that were eating like kings and shit! Their time was up.

I pulled my phone out and logged onto the D.O.C website so I could look my favorite enemy up. I smiled when I noticed that his good time date had gotten updated. He was getting out fourteen days earlier. I was happier than his family was. Then, I stared at his picture with hate. He had a lil' smirk on his face. It was like he was taunting me.

"We gon' see if you smirking in that fuckin' casket, bitch." I gripped my phone like it was his neck.

Marcellus Allen

Chapter 16
Juice

"Who keeps fuckin' calling you at five o'clock in the morning !"

I woke up to being shoved by my bitch and her complaining in my ear. It took seconds for me to snap back into reality. I had a dream of Anna's dead body talking to me. She was standing over me with blood leaking out of her head, asking me why her and her child had to die. Her lifeless eyes stared into mine, freezing my soul and preventing me from answering her.

"How the fuck am I supposed to know?" I grabbed my phone and saw a weird ass number blowing me up.

"Who the hell is this?" I answered ready to flip out.

I sat up and listened to an operator explain that I had a free five minute call from Latoya. Her dumb ass was in booking. I accepted the call.

"Baby daddy, I need you!" She yelled immediately.

"Yo, what yo dumb ass in jail for? And what you calling me for? I ain't yo' nigga." I spazzed.

"But I'm your daughter's mother and I need you! Please!" She sounded desperate.

"What do you want, Latoya? And where the fuck is my daughter?" I got hot thinking about my angel.

"I need you to come bail me out. I'm in here for domestic violence."

I busted out laughing. "You a dumb bitch and tell yo nigga to come post yo bail."

"He snitched on me and hung up when I called him!"

The operator said we had one minute left.

"I'll be there." I said, then hung up while she was trying to say something.

I got out the bed and started getting dressed. The whole time Brittney was mean muggin' the shit out of me with her arms folded. I acted like I didn't feel the heat and just kept on getting dressed. I'd forgotten to ask the dumb bitch how much the bail was. *Anything more than this and she staying in there.* I promised myself while pulling five bands from the safe.

"So, that bitch calls and you go running?" Brittney finally spoke her mind.

"Only thing I run for is to kill a nigga and you know that. At the end of the day, she's still my baby mama and she needs me right now." I checked her.

"And? Just cause you got a baby with the bitch don't mean you're her Superman." She rolled her eyes like all bitches did.

I exhaled then sat down on the bed next to her. I knew she got really insecure when it came to Latoya. She didn't give two fucks about Naughty or any other bitch. But Latoya was another story. She knew our history and all the shit we'd been through growing up together. She really felt in her heart that Latoya could steal me forever.

"Listen, y'all are both my baby moms. Loyalty is loyalty no matter if we're together or not. I'm not about to be one of those fake niggas that leaves their loved ones in jail for dead. I gotta die a real nigga just like my brotha did. All my homies would leave their bitches in jail but not me. I might need y'all to be some real bitches for me in the future. That's where niggas go wrong, then cry when their bitches do 'em foul."

I knew she felt where I was coming from. It was all in her eyes, plus she got silent for a whole minute.

"But what if she ends up being a fake bitch when you need her the most?"

I smiled then kissed her on the lips. "Then, I'ma still have you."

"What if I turn into a fake bitch, too?" She was trying hard to knock down my real nigga walls. I got up and turned around when I got to the door. She was still staring at me for an answer.

"Then, I'ma have to live with the fact that I chose wrong. That I put my faith in the wrong people. But either way, when I die they gon' bury me a real nigga. Kiss my daughter for me."

I left the spot without saying another word. I knew that no matter how much real shit I did that couldn't make a fake muthafucka a real one. I was young but far from being naive` when it came to this street shit. But until a muthafucka showed me disloyalty, I would forever give them my loyalty. I just prayed that whenever the betrayal came that it wouldn't cut me too deep. I knew what I'd signed up for. I was in this shit till death called my name. Literally.

It only took me twenty minutes to get downtown to the Justice Center and post her bail but had to wait over an hour for her to get released. While I waited, I hopped on the net to see what the streets were saying. The fuck nigga with the dreads didn't die but took two to the stomach. His name was Wuan. I found it comical how they were praising the pussy for taking some bullets. I was gon' make him a hood legend when I caught up with him again. I found out a bitch got hit in the thigh, too. *She'll be alright.*

Latoya finally came out and hopped in the truck with an attitude. She didn't look like she'd just gotten out of jail. She looked like she'd had a long night at the club.

"What's good, jail bird?" I laughed at her.

"It's not funny, Davontae. I can't believe this shit!" She started to get animated.

I pulled out the lot, wanting to get far away from them crackerz as possible. We went a few minutes in silence, then she broke it.

"Thank you for coming to get me. I appreciate it," she said.

"You good, tell me what happened."

"Long story short, I caught him cheating and whooped his ass. I busted that niggas shit right in front of the house Then, we started fighting. Somebody called the cops. He gon' tell the cops I hit him first!"

"You fell in love with a snitch." I started laughing.

"Yo, where my daughter at?" I lost my sense of humor real fast.

"She should be in her room."

"You better hope so." I spat.

I picked up the pace. I wanted to hurry up and see my seed. I got mad at the thought of her living under the same roof as a snitch.

"This can't keep happening around my daughter, fo'real." I told her.

"I know, Davontae."

"First time she see that shit, we gon' have a real problem. She not gon' grow up traumatized from seeing her mama getting her ass whooped. The very first time it happens, I'm pulling up. It's gon' be guns up fo'real. On my brotha. And if you gotta problem with it, then you can get it too." I turned on Finesse2Tymes. There was nothing else to say.

Ten minutes later, we pulled up to her house and I turned the music off. I was still hot but my temper died down a lil' bit.

"You owe me three bands, too. I ain't got a problem shooting you some bread but I ain't paying for another nigga to put you in jail. I don't know what y'all bitches see in these snitches anyway."

"Whatever, I'll get you your lil' money. I'm already tired of hearing yo' voice, damn." She shot back, then grabbed the door handle.

My hand shot to her face, gripping her jaw bones. Now I was mad. "Watch yo' mouth. Don't forget who your fuckin' talkin' to, bitch. I ain't that cop calling nigga you've been playing house with. I was sleep with my bitch when you woke me up. I got out of my bed for yo' smart mouthed ass. Now go get my daughter." I growled.

"I'm surprised she let you come and get me. We both know how she's all insecure and shit when it comes to me." She flipped her hair and smiled at me.

"Don't nobody dictate my moves and you know that better than anybody. Regardless, if she trippin' or not, I'm never gon' leave you for dead. Loyalty is loyalty no matter what and I explained it to her. But with that last stunt you pulled, you're walking a fine line, tramp."

She sucked her teeth. "That was not that serious and you know it. All I said was I'd start dropping Lisa off at your mother's house 'cause I didn't want you to end up killing Rocky. It ain't like I tried to keep her away from you or somethin'."

"Still, I ain't like that shit."

"I'm sorry, baby daddy." She started playing with my dreads and then rubbing on my neck.

My dick started rising. I couldn't remember the last time I'd felt her throat. "You better get in the house before he come out here and beat yo ass."

132

"Fuck that cheating ass nigga. He probably in there on the phone with another bitch anyway. I wanna suck yo dick while he's right there in the house." She pulled my meat out and started massaging it.

"Shit, I'm not about to stop you." I leaned my seat back and enjoyed the show.

I kept my eyes glued to their front door in case her bitch ass nigga came storming out. I had the Mac I'd just used on the floor and wouldn't hesitate to pop another pussy with it.

She was sucking the shit out of my dick, slurping and moaning while she did it. My eyes rolled back a few times.

"Damn, I forgot how good you suck dick." I moaned out.

She tried to say something but I pushed her head down not interested in her words at all. Soon as I got ready to blast off, I saw the door fly open and Rocky stick his head out. Then, he slammed it shut. I used my hand to speed her neck up.

"Ahhh!" I shot a load in her mouth less than a minute later.

She swallowed then wiped her mouth with a wicked smile on her face.

"Yo nigga came out here." I told her.

"What! When!" She started tripping out, wiping her face hella fast with panic in her eyes.

I busted out laughing while I pulled my pants up. The stupid ass look on her face was priceless. She was just talking bad on the nigga, then started acting like she couldn't afford to lose him. *Bitches ain't shit!*

"A couple minutes ago. Here he come again." I peeped game on how he went and put a hoody on.

I picked the Mac up ready to bust that Muthafucka at the first sign of aggression. I could see the shape of a pistol as he marched down the stairs. He was ready to die over some pussy that didn't belong to him.

"Please don't provoke him, Juice." She must've noticed it too.

"You better go remind him who I am then." I was gripping the iron getting madder with each step he took.

She bounced out on a mission. Soon as the door opened, they

started yelling at the same time.

"Bitch, what the fuck you doing in that nigga's car!"

"Fuck you nigga! You left me in jail!"

I sat back and enjoyed the show. The shit was comical to me. I wished I had some popcorn. After a few minutes of the antics, I got bored with it and just wanted to see my daughter. I rolled the window down and honked the horn.

"What you want nigga! What the fuck you still doing here?" Rocky yelled like he was tough.

Let it go Juice he just emotional right now. My conscience told me.

"I'm just trying to see my daughter fam." I kept it cool.

"Well, she sleep nigga! And didn't we tell you not to come over here no more?" He spat.

I couldn't believe he wanted to play tough 'cause he had a pistol on him. Emotional or not, I didn't allow nobody to play with my gangsta or my seed. I hopped out and rushed toward the nigga like I was the Terminator. My hand rested on my waist just begging his pussy ass to reach in his hoody. I was gon' really give the neighbors something to call the police for.

"You better lower yo voice when talkin' to me, you bitch ass nigga. I put niggas in the ground fo'real." I spit out flame as I walked up.

"And nigga? You think they stopped making guns when you bought yours?"

"Juice NO! Don't do it!" Latoya jumped in front of him.

She'd just swallowed my nut and now she was ready to take a bullet for him. Hood bitches were weird like that.

"Watch out, bitch." He shoved her to the side "What you wanna do, nigga?" He yelled trying to pump himself up. He was so lovestruck that it was pathetic. I wanted to fall on the ground and laugh at his bitch ass. But he issued a direct challenge and by the code of the streets, it had to be accepted.

Whack! Whack!

I hit him in the face with the steel, making him crumble to the concrete. I decided to spare his soul from the fire 'cause my daughter really liked the guy. He was really a nice nigga. Plus, I really didn't wanna body the nigga in broad day with all them nosey ass neighbors. Her head game wasn't worth a life sentence. At least not to me.

"This the last time I'ma spare you, on my dead brotha," I pulled a .22 from his hoody then kicked him for disrespecting the game with that lil' ass pistol. "Don't play with me again or hit her in front of my daughter and we good."

"Just leave, Juice!" Latoya yelled.

I stared at Rocky squirming on the ground, bleeding every where like a real bitch. I knew at that moment I'd made the right choice 'cause some cowards weren't worth the bullets.

"Shut up, bitch, before I change my mind and get y'all bunkbeds at the coroner's office." I mugged her up and down scaring her to death.

I hopped in the truck and left before my demons got the best of me and I fed the reaper. That shit was not how I had planned my morning at all. The streets were crazy like that, though.

Marcellus Allen

Chapter 17
Juice

After I left from Latoya's spot, I went straight to McDonald's off of 82nd street and ordered everything they had on the breakfast menu. Busting a nut and having to pistol whip a sucka-for-love, had a real nigga hungry as a muthafucka. I was still laughing about the whole situation when my phone rung.

It was Gunna.

"What's up with it, gang?" I answered with a mouth full of food.

"Aye, where yo' hot ass at?" He asked.

"Eating at McDonalds. Nigga tell me why I just had to pistol whip that sucka nigga Rocky over the bitch." I busted out laughing.

"Fuck all that. You and Omar just went viral for that stunt y'all pulled in the Ville."

"Nigga, what?" I felt my stomach drop.

"Some bitches were recording y'all argue from across the street. Then, y'all left and a minute later somebody yelled the set out before y'all got to bustin'. It don't show y'all faces during the shooting though, just when y'all leave. Muthafuckaz been on Facebook going crazy too, dry snitching and shit."

I shoulda took them bitches' phones!

"Fuck it, it is what it is. We already got the town on fire so we just gon' finish our meal and get this money. We already got the two drops in so ain't no point in falling back now." I could already taste all the money waiting on me, no stopping.

"Blood, you already know I'm with it! I don't give a fuck about being hot or none of that shit. We gon' drop them rats, then step our game up, period. Let faggot ass gangstas worry about all that other shit, on the gang." He spat.

I already knew what he was gon' say before he said it. Gunna didn't give a fuck about nothing and that's what made him so dangerous. I hung up on him, then found the video on Facebook. It wasn't hard to find. It was the only thing poppin' on the net at nine o'clock in the morning. It was so many muthafuckaz dry snitchin' and talking shit on there. It was crazy. We had at least a hundred different death threats but that was nothing. Everybody talked tough on the net until dem choppa bullets started picking them apart. *Pussies.*

I didn't like the fact that my truck was in the video. That was a good enough reason for the pigs to pull me over and I couldn't afford that. After giving it much thought, I knew exactly where to get another whip from.

Twenty minutes later, I was pulling in the condos that I lived with Naughty in. It felt weird being there after not being there for weeks. Shit, we'd barely even spoken to each other, just a few angry texts. I found her Lexus parked in her spot and felt a lil' rush. *I do miss that bitch.* I swapped cars and peeled out the lot before I gave in. At the red light is when the shit really hit me. The whole whip smelled like Chanel perfume, her favorite scent. That shit made me miss her ten times more. I pulled my phone out, ready to give in. *Naw fuck that!* I shook my head, letting my pride get the best of me.

45 minutes later

"I swear to the gang! This shit was a scene straight from Cheaters. I was just waiting on the cameras!" I told Mask, then we busted out laughing again.

For the past ten minutes, I'd been breaking down all the triv with Latoya and her wack ass baby daddy. We both found the shit hella funny.

Mask passed me the Backwood. "I would've popped his bitch ass on the gang. Fuck all that." He was dead serious.

I hit the exotic weed a few times, letting it calm my nerves. "Pop 'em for what? The nigga is far from a threat. That's a pointless body that don't count."

"'Cause suckaz kill over bitches all the time, that's why. Love mixed with some good pussy makes cowards ready for war all the time. We should just get 'em out the way right now."

I felt where he was coming from and knew there was some merit to what he was saying but I wasn't worried about it. I just couldn't see the nigga actually pulling a trigga, not even to save his own life.

Plus, I didn't feel like having to deal with Latoya and everything that came with it. The shit wasn't worth it.

I waved my hand at him brushing it off. "Man, fuck all that. We got bigger shit to worry about right now. We gotta get at them Goonie niggas, holla at Pete and kill two snitches." Just the thought of all of it was blowing my high.

"Let's focus on the most important thing first, our money. Once we got the money and the power, everybody else gon' bow down. Let's get our connect, then kill everybody else." He suggested.

What he said made complete sense to me.

"Well, we already know where he at right now. Shit, we know his whole schedule. What you wanna do?" I tested my nigga's gangsta.

He cracked a lil' smile. "Say less, we sliding tonight."

Right when I was getting ready to respond with something slick, my phone started going off. I knew it was Naughty by the ringtone. I cracked a smile. *It ain't gon' be that easy.* I hit ignore.

Hours later

"You really think O-Dawg gon' come through with the plug?" Mask asked out of nowhere.

We were sitting in Naughty's whip, parked in the P.C.C parking lot off of 42nd and Killingsworth. We'd been there for over an hour waiting on the night classes to end. We'd gotten word that Ralo was taking classes trying to get his G.E. D and become a barber. His mama could lay both certificates in the casket with him as far as I was concerned. He'd done way too much dirt in the streets to even think about turning his life around. It amazed me that he actually thought shit was gon' work out like that. I knew plenty of snitches walking around Portland real brave but telling on O-Dawg was different. He had too much pull and too much money.

"Yeah, he gon' come through. What kinda shit you on?" I responded. I'd never even thought twice about the shit. His word was gold.

He shrugged. "You know I don't trust shit. I just don't wanna be nobody's pawn on their chess board." He replied.

I was too busy replying to Naughty's texts and watching the lot to entertain that nigga's foolishness.

I'll do whatever it takes to prove my loyalty to you.

We'll see. I wrote back.

"Yo, lover boy? Here the nigga comes." Mask stopped my thoughts of Naughty.

I stuffed the phone in my pocket, then started looking out of the window. I spotted the rat walking out of the building with a white chick on his side. He had a smile on his face like he didn't have a care in the world. Like he didn't put a nigga he used to get money with, in a jail cell. His happiness infuriated me to my core.

"I hope this white bitch ain't leaving with him." I growled.

"I wouldn't give a fuck if they were glued to each other. She can get it too." Mask spat as he slid on his ski mask.

My eyes burned with fury as they walked through the lot. I wanted to body the nigga so bad. "Naw, we can't crush an innocent white bitch, that's too much heat. We already too hot right now, trust me."

"Well, she about to get traumatized then. She gon' witness black on black crime close up. I bet you she gon' go back to white boys after this shit."

My nigga was hell bent on poppin' his top so I knew something had to give. Either she was dyin' too or not, but Ralo wasn't gon' make it. I started visualizing it in my mind. I was ready.

"If they get in the car together, we gon' run up and slump 'em in his seat. All she gon' be able to tell the pigs is two muthafuckaz with masks on killed her boyfriend. That ain't shit."

"Say less." He replied.

We watched like predators of the night as they approached a black Nissan. Ralo opened the door for her like a real sucka, kissed her then walked off. Soon as she drove out, I eased the Lexus out of the spot and crept behind the rat. Right when he got to his car, he turned around and spotted us. I knew he felt the fear of his past catching up to him. The look on his face said it all. Mask bounced out and was on him instantly.

"O-Dawg told me to tell you what's up nigga!" I stuck my head out the window.

"I'm not with that shit no more, bro." He replied

"Tell the devil to get yo snitch ass a barber chair when you get there, pussy!"

Boom! Boom! Boom!

Mask opened his chest up and he crumbled to the ground. He stood over him for a closed casket. *Boom! Boom!* Two head shots, then he hopped back in the whip. "Rats don't deserve open caskets, on the gang." He vowed as we peeled out.

"Fuck that nigga and his family," Was all I had to say before I turned on G-Herbo.

Marcellus Allen

Chapter 18
Naughty

Just when I was starting to believe that Juice was really done fuckin' with me, the nigga comes and swaps me cars out of nowhere. Street niggas don't let random bitches push their whips, only wifey gets that privilege. His ass knew what he was doing when he did that. He knew he was gon' climb right back into my head with that shit. I immediately started blowing his phone up. The nigga had the nerve to send me straight to voicemail and he didn't even have one set up! He had me fucked up. I sent him multiple texts cussing him out. He wrote me back talking about he was busy and he'll get at me. I did end up talking to him later that night for an hour, though. But that was three days ago and we still hadn't seen each other. I was fed up with that shit! He was gon' have to get it together.

"Bitch, I'm not going in tonight. I might not ever go back to work. I'm tired of shaking my ass." I vented to Jessie. We were at my condo getting ready to go to work and for some reason I just wasn't feeling the shit.

"Whatever bitch, soon as Juice tap that ass you'll be ready to shake it again," she said, then started laughing.

"Naw, I'm serious girl," I sat down on the couch and checked to see if Juice had texted me. "I feel like if I don't get out of there real soon, then I'll never be able to do it. I want my clothing line, I want a family, and I want it now. I'm done clubbing, stripping and all that fast life shit."

"Damn, that was deep. You really need yo pussy sucked on."

We both busted out laughing this time. There I was pouring out my heart and all she could think about was my pussy.

"Well, since you're so focused on my pussy, I did let Jamar eat my pussy last week." I confessed.

"Bitch, what! How that happen? You're a thot, fo'real." She jumped on the couch all excited.

I told her the story, play by play. How Jamar got a new house and wanted me to see it so I would feel comfortable letting Lil' Jamar stay there. When I got there, he started selling me dreams and shit about our future and our family. He eventually got me wet so I let him eat me out. I wouldn't let him hit it though. I couldn't let it be that easy.

"Bitch, you scandalous!" She yelled while laughing way too hard. I was impersonating how desperate he was acting over the pussy.

"That's what he get for doing scandalous shit. I don't know what I'ma do with that nigga. It look like me and Juice are going to work things out."

"You better figure it out before Juice crazy ass finds out. If he even think you're giving his pussy away, he gon' go ape shit and you know it. He gon' kill both of y'all and me too for knowing about it." She actually looked scared.

I sucked my teeth. "That nigga always saying he'll never chase a bitch or beef with a nigga over one, including me. He stay talking bad on niggas for doing that."

She rolled her eyes extra dramatically. "All these extra hard street niggas be preaching that shit until it happen to them. They be the worst ones. And they stay killing over a bitch, then covering it up to make it look like something else. C'mon, mami, you know this." She lectured me. And I definitely did. But I just couldn't see Juice trippin' out like that.

"He don't be trippin' like that, Jes."

"Bitch, him and his crazy ass homies done shot half of Portland in the last month! You ain't been seeing all the shit on Facebook? They been wildin' out for nothing. And the streets are saying that everybody that snitched on O-Dawg has been getting killed recently."

"And what that mean?" I already knew the answer though.

"They started getting shot after they posted that picture in the visiting room. Shit, that's probably why he still riding around in yo car."

My mind went to the bullet hole by the trunk. But she wasn't saying shit I didn't already know. What she didn't know was, I was the one that linked him and O-Dawg back up. I knew he was out there on one, but I knew it had to be a reason for it.

"That has nothing to do with me, though, and I thought you liked Davontae?"

"I love y'all together. That's why I'm telling yo' stupid ass not to start acting like no thot." She claimed.

"We're on break!"

"Aint no such thing to niggas like him. You're his property, period."

"Should I just tell him?" I asked.

"If you wanna die."

We went back and forth for another thirty minutes until it was time for her to get to work. I stayed my ass home like I said I was. Fuck stripping! I got out my scrap book and started working on some new designs I had in my head. "Fuck this shit!" I tossed my pen in frustration then picked my phone up.

"What's the triv?" My nigga answered the phone like he always did. Just hearing his voice had me feeling some type of way. *Damn I love this nigga.*

"You got a real ass bitch and a step-son over here that wanna know if your fuckin' with us or not! That's the triv!" I spazzed on him, letting my emotions get the best of me.

He started chuckling then said, "I miss you too baby."

"Do you really?" I was ready to cry.

"Yeah, I do, and where my son at? I wanna holla at him really quick."

Oh shit. "Uhh. He's been at Jamar's house the last couple of days," I told the truth. He went silent for a full minute and I could feel the heat through the phone. "Hello? Are you still there, Davontae?"

"So, you been over the nigga house, huh? Did he try and get at you? And don't lie." He finally spoke.

I had a flashback of Jamar eating my pussy on the counter. "Kinda, but it's not like that, Davontae." I vowed.

"Bitch, you know you ain't supposed to be inside no niggas house without me being there. I wouldn't give a fuck if it was the pope. Don't call me till you got my son with you. And don't make me kill you and that nigga. I don't fuck with his homies anyway."

He growled then hung up.

It felt good knowing that he still loved me but damn he was nuts. *Jessie was right.* It was no way in hell I was gonna tell him what happened. Fuck that. For all that tough guy shit he spoke, it was clear he was dangerously in love with me. Hearing him get so jealous like that, had my pussy throbbing. I leaned back on the couch, pulled my panties to the side and found my love bottom.

The next day I pulled up to Jamar's new house off of 189th and Powell. I didn't know how he could afford the three-bedroom house after only being out of jail for less than sixty days but it was fly as hell. I walked past two different types of Benz's parked by the curve in front of his house. *Who over here?* I knocked on the door with an attitude. *This nigga bet not have no ratchet ass bitches around my son!*

Jamar opened the door wearing only some basketball shorts with a wood hanging out of his mouth. I got stuck staring at his muscles and forgot about my suspicions.

"What's up, baby? Why you ain't call first?" He asked with a smirk on his face.

That shit snapped me out of my muscular daze. "I didn't know I had to." I folded my arms and snapped my neck.

"So you're pushin' his whip now, huh?" I caught a glimpse of anger in his eyes.

"Move." I pushed him out of my way as I rushed inside.

The smell of weed was strong and the speakers were blasting some Youngboy NBA song. I heard a few niggas voices coming from the front room as I speed walked.

Jamar was right behind me laughing like something was funny. When I walked in the front room, I saw Ray-Ray and D-Roc sitting on the couch counting up more money that I'd ever seen. They had piles of money on the table and one the floor. It had to at least be a million dollars, at least. My son was sitting in front of the big screen playing some shooting video game. He even had a lil' stack of money in front of him.

"Naughty, what's up baby girl?" Ray-Ray had a smile on his face. I'd be smiling too if I had all that money.

"What's crackin' lil' sis?" D-Roc asked. We did not have no brother-sister relationship.

"Hey y'all, and why do y'all have my son in here like he's some type of drug dealer or something?" I replied.

My son's head snapped around at the sound of my voice. "Mama!" He jumped up hella excited to see me. He ran toward me, then turned around to pick his money up, then came back.

"Hey baby!" I lifted him up in the air, kissing him all over. It was the first time we'd been apart for days and I missed him like crazy.

"Look mama, we got money for yo' clothes store!" He shoved his money in my face. That really touched my heart. *Jamar know what he doing.*

"Stop babying him. Go play yo game lil' nigga." Jamar took him out of my hands.

"Yo, how much I gotta invest in yo clothes? I'm trying to go legit anyways." Ray-Ray asked.

"On Crip." D-Roc agreed.

"Don't start that crab shit, bitch." Ray-Ray said.

"Shut up, slob."

Jamar wrapped his arms around me. "You gon' answer his question or what?"

I didn't know what to say. That was the last thing I was expecting to be asked. Shit, I didn't even know exactly how much I needed.

"Shit, I don't know." I shrugged. "Probably like twenty or twenty-five thousand."

They both started laughing on the couch, hella hard like we were watching Kevin Hart or something. I didn't know if the weed had them trippin' or if it was me.

"That's it? I spent that on my bitch last week in the Bahamas. Yo, why you ain't been gave that shit to her?" Ray-Ray clowned.

"It's gon' cost way more than that. She just ain't did the numbers on it. But I ain't giving her shit long as she's driving the next nigga's car." He said with jealousy dripping from his words.

Ray-Ray went to the window then whistled being hella

dramatic. "So, you pushin' the Escalade, huh? It's a few years old too. You got a real boss in yo face and you wanna settle for the help?" He downplayed Juice.

"Why are y'all worried about who's dick I'm fuckin' on?" I spat with major attitude.

"Watch yo' mouth in front of my son." Jamar grabbed me by the wrist. "C'mon, we need to talk." He yanked me all the way to his bedroom.

"Let me go." I snatched away from him after we got inside.

I was hella pissed off. I didn't like how they were disrespecting Juice in front of me. And I really didn't like how they were dangling my dream in my face like that.

"Why you driving that nigga's car? You know that shit is disrespectful bringing that shit over here."

"How? It ain't like y'all are beefing." I shot back.

"Our homies don't see eye to eye but fuck all that. I'm over here putting on for your dream, then you pull up in that shit?" He was really getting mad.

I could see where he was coming from when he put it like that. His pride had took a big hit.

"I'm sorry, I didn't know." I gave in and apologized. The anger in his eyes started to melt away like that.

"Here, I got somethin' for you." He walked away, going to his closet.

I knew he was about to pull out something out of there that I was going to love. I was expecting some fly ass heels or maybe a nice necklace. But what he turned around with, I was not expecting. I screamed my head off in joy as I ran toward him. He had bought me the newest Berkin bag. The exact one I'd been dreaming about. The bag hit his pockets for more than ten thousand.

"Oh my God! Thank you!" I gave him a quick kiss then snatched the bag from him. I held it in the air, kissed it, rubbed it, then modeled with it. I fell instantly in love with it.

"I love you ma, fo'real." He said while he stared in my eyes with the most sincerity I'd ever seen.

"Do you really?"

148

He took the bag from me then sat me down on the edge of the bed. "More than anything, I promise," He kneeled in front of me. "I know I fucked up in the past but I've grown from that. I want us to be a family, get married and have more kids. I wanna give you the world."

I didn't know what to say. My emotions were all fucked up and all over the place. "It's not that easy Jamar, I'm still figuring things out with Juice. I don't wanna play either one of y'all." I kept it real.

"Sshh, stop talkin'." He pushed me back on the bed then started pulling my pants off. I was gonna stop him but I figured I'd already crossed the line, so fuck it.

Before I knew it, his tongue had found my clit and I was moaning my head off. I don't know what kinda pussy eating books he'd read in jail but man did they teach him something! He knew all the right moves and spots to hit. In less than ten minutes, he'd gotten me to cum twice and I was working on my third when somebody started pounding on the door.

"Yo Jay!" It was Ray-Ray.

"What nigga!" Jamar yelled with my juices dripping from his face.

"C'mon nigga, we gotta go! Code red!"

"What the fuck?" He jumped up with an attitude.

"The nigga Rico just got out and he's already shot up one of our spots."

"Fuck! Alright, here I come."

"It's okay, I got errands to run anyways." I said before he could start making excuses.

"Think about what I said. We'll talk later."

"Okay." I got up, grabbed my bag then left before he tried to hold me hostage.

By the way they were rushing out of there, it let me know that whoever Rico was he was a real problem. I knew I'd heard the name before but couldn't remember where from.

"You have fun with your daddy?" I asked my son as I drove into the traffic.

"Yup!" He was really excited in the backseat.

"Did you miss me? 'Cause it don't seem like you missed your mama."

"I missed you mama! Mama, can I have McDonald's please? I got money." He held his lil' stack in the air.

I nodded then busted out laughing. He was already ready to start blowing his money. My thoughts switched to Jamar and all his promises to me. He was saying everything that I wanted to hear and some. The problem was that I wanted to hear those words from Juice. But for some reason, my dreams and goals were not a priority for him. He was too caught up in the streets to think about anything else. I still felt kinda bad for letting Jamar eat me out twice, though. But at the same time, I knew he was still fuckin' on his baby mama, so what's the difference? At least, I wasn't out being a hoe like he'd done numerous times. I grabbed my phone and called Faith. I needed to fill her in and get some golddigging advice. These niggas had my head all fucked up.

Chapter 19
Juice

I was chilling at my mama's spot spending time with both my daughters when I got the call about Nipsey Hussle.

"Yo, they saying the nigga Nipsey just got smoked in his own hood out there in L.A." Mask told me over the phone.

"How the fuck that happen?" I was dumbfounded. I couldn't understand how a nigga that much love had so get killed in his own hood.

"I don't know, word is some snitch nigga from his hood crushed him 'cause he told 'em he can't post at his store with bad paperwork."

"What the fuck! That sound like some shit one of these rat muthafuckaz down here would do."

"Now, you know this gangsta rat shit is universal." He spoke the ghetto gospel.

All I could do was shake my head at hearing that ho shit. Real niggas weren't supposed to get took out the game by rats. I didn't give a fuck what set you claimed!

"Yo' I'm crushin' the first snitch I catch out in North-East, on me. I don't give a fuck if they told on a turtle, I'm smashin' 'em." I vowed from the heart.

"I feel you gang, but we just killed three of them for the cause and we still ain't heard from the plug. Niggas is starting to feel some type of way."

I could hear the anger behind his words I didn't fault him for it but I didn't feel the same way. I knew O-Dawg's word was gold. He told me to give him a week or so, so that's what I was gonna do.

It had been five days since Gunna and Flash caught Olay coming out of the beauty salon and left her slumped in her car. "At least she gon' look hella fly in her casket. Whoever did her hair had her shit looking right." Gunna said making us laugh later that night when we all met up at Omar's spot.

I didn't feel a drop of sympathy for her like I did with Anna. Anna was a casualty of war. Olay had helped the crackerz bury her baby dad alive. She lucky I wasn't there 'cause I would've kept shooting until her head fell off her shoulder. But I had bigger problems to deal with, bigger heads to shoot off. Word on the streets was that I had a price on my head and a lotta suckaz wanted to collect it. I already knew Pistol Pete's bitch ass was the one who put the bag out. So we were gonna kill that nigga on sight then shoot up his so called shooters.

Me and Gunna had slid by Faith's house a few different times hoping to see his car parked outside but he was never there. I knew he was smarter than that but niggas always lost common sense when it came to pussy. I knew she knew his where abouts though. I planned on having a chat with her when I got tired of looking for the nigga.

Then, to make matters worse, the nigga Rico had gotten out of jail for some attempts he was fighting and came home trippin'. He was the main killa for the Goonies but I was gon' show him who the real goon was. He had already popped a few niggas from the Gas team and sent word that I was next. But I was gon' remind the whole city who the fuck I am.

Soon as the heat died down, I planned on putting the flame on niggas. They were all claiming they were lions, bears and tigers. Well, I was about to go hunting and then hang their heads on my mantel. As soon as the informants stopped dropping our names to the pigs. Me and my niggas were the main suspects for Olay, Phats, Anna and Ralo. That picture I took with O-Dawg was fuckin' us over.

I told Mask to be patient and I would hit him up later. I had to get the kids ready to go to Bullweinkos with Naughty and my step-son. We'd been talking a lot over the past week and decided to try and work the shit out. I slid over to her spot the other night and dicked her down like crazy. Then, she woke me up the next morning talking about officially living together and shit. I don't know why her and Brittney kept pushing that relationship shit on me. I was only 21 and was far from ready to settle down. I loved my bitches and would kill for both of them but they could miss me with that monogamous shit.

"What's good, gang?" Gunna answered the phone.

"Shit, about to link up with Naughty and take these kids out. I'm on some family shit today." I told him

"Nigga yo' square ass just wanna be all up under Naughty, stop lyin' on the kids." He started laughing.

"Whateva nigga, you hear about the nigga Nipsey Hussle?"

"Yeah, I been hearing about the shit since I woke up. Muthafuckaz been calling me about it like I'm supposed to care about some dead crab 'cause he was a rapper." He spat.

"You hella disrespectful, gang. That nigga was doing a lot for our culture. It don't matter that he was Crip. We don't even be beefin' with the Sixties."

"And? Nigga we ain't no fuckin' black activists so that shit don't matter. We just killed a few blacks in the last month. So, you can keep that black lives matter shit to yourself and focus on getting that connect." He really sounded offended.

I stared at the phone for a second trying to control my anger. Sometimes Gunna didn't know how to turn it down or watch how he talked to people.

"You shut yo bitch ass up and focus on building up our movement." I hung up giving him something to think about.

I sent O-Dawg a text asking him what's the status? I had a pack of wolves that needed to be fed before they started hunting again. I was trying to get us away from all that robbin' and contract killing. But if I didn't produce a plate real soon, they were gonna go find their own meals. Shit, I was too. I couldn't hold on to the lil' money I had in my safe forever.

"Daddy, grandma said come eat!" My daughter Lisa busted in the room shouting.

"A'ight, c'mon baby." I picked her up then headed out. She looked like Latoya so much it was crazy. We'd exchanged texts a couple times since I had to smack her baby daddy with the heat. She thanked me for not detaching his soul from his body. But her nigga wasn't as appreciative. He was over there talking that searching for revenge shit! But she said he didn't even own another gun. The first time he brought one in the house though, I was gon' kill 'em, period.

Marcellus Allen

Chapter 20
Juice

"What's good, baby?" I kissed Naughty on the lips after I got the kids settled in the backseat.

"Hi daddy, how you feeling?" She pulled out the driveway starting the forty-five minute ride to Wilsonville, Oregon. How I was really feeling couldn't be spoken about in front of the kids or to my bitch. Real gangstaz kept all complaining and their emotions to themselves. We dealt with it internally and got the job done by any means necessary, period.

"You look beautiful, baby." I said instead.

"Thank you." She smiled like all woman did when complimented. "But you didn't answer my question, and I need to fix up your dreads, too."

"I'm good." I lied then checked my phone for a text from O-Dawg. There wasn't one. I was becoming too anxious.

"You know what happened that ain't cool?"

"What?" She asked.

"Some nigga killed Nipsey Hussle at his own store out there in L.A. That shit got me hot right now." I spat.

"Oh my God. I know, that's so sad. And it was his own friend that did it. Have you seen the video?"

"Naw, I ain't seen no video yet."

She pulled out her phone then handed it to me with the video playing. I stared at the screen with more hate than I expected. My demons spoke to me every time I pressed replay. I couldn't believe the nigga actually kicked him in the head!

"Snitch bitch muthafucka!" I yelled out.

"Juice! The kids." She checked me.

I didn't give a fuck what she was talking about. I was hot! I turned around and looked at the kids really quick. Jamar was playing his game unaffected. He was used to it. Both my daughters were staring at me, though. I turned back to the video while Naughty put on some soft ass R&B that I didn't wanna hear. I was already gonna smash the first rat I caught slippin' but now I was gonna destroy and demoralize him. *Bitch ass nigga!*

My hand was shaking just dyin' to grip a pistol. Watching it made me think about my brotha getting smoked in front of me and my mom's.

"That's enough baby." Naughty took the phone from me.

It didn't matter though 'cause the shit was burned into my mind forever. I hooked my phone up to the stereo, turning that soft shit off. I put on 'I Don't Stress' by Nipsey and turnt it all the way up. Naughty looked at me with a crazy look but I didn't give a fuck.

"I don't stress out nigga, poke my chest out nigga, wait for my show to bring my best out nigga"

I rapped with my nigga for the next twenty minutes really feeling what the fuck he was spittin'. I didn't care what color his flag was, he was a real nigga. I didn't beef with Crips anyways. I just hated the Crip that killed my brotha with so much passion that I stayed away from them niggas. But my gun didn't discriminate at all. I was an everybody killer fo'real.

A few hours later, I was sitting at the table watching the kids jump inside the playpen having the time of their lives. They'd been at it for hours and were showing no signs of slowing down. I just smiled and took it all in 'cause I rarely had time to do shit like this. The streets wouldn't allow me to slow down or take any breaks. And with all the new funk I handled, I knew my time was gon' really be short. Shit, I knew it was a good chance I wouldn't live through the year.

"Baby we need to talk." Naughty said the words that no man ever wanted to hear. She came and sat next to me looking like she had some deep shit to get off of her chest.

"A'ight, what you wanna talk about?"

"Us of course," She smiled then kissed me on the lips. "We need to figure out what we're doing and where are we going from here."

"Not this shit again." I slapped my forehead.

"Yeah, this shit again and I'm adding more to it, too."

"What now, Naughty?"

"I want you to leave all this street shit alone now. It ain't getting us nowhere. Every time I turn around, either you done killed somebody or somebody wanna kill you. It's time for both of us to move on and build up something that can't be tore down. You can help me pay for my store and clothing line and I can help you do whatever."

I stared in her eyes and saw the sincerity in them. She was so serious. I had to stop myself from laughing in her face. I was never leaving the streets alone and I thought she knew that.

"Yo, you been watching that Dr. Phil bullshit again or what? You ashamed to be a stripper or somethin'? Where the fuck this shit coming from? You must got some square nigga in yo ear." I spat.

"I'm not ashamed of nothing I've had to do to feed my son, nigga," She started moving her hands around and snapping her neck. "But I am done doing the shit and I don't care how you feel about it. And I'm done sharing my nigga too. You not about to keep bed hopping from me to Brittney to whoever the fuck else your fuckin'! Either be the man me and my son deserves or get out of our lives." She spat venom at me.

All I could do was look at her like she'd lost her mind and try to figure out where all this was coming from. *She must be on her period.*

"Baby listen, I'm working on some shit that's gon' change our lives forever. Once I get it done, you can stop dancing and do whatever you wanna do. Don't leave me 'cause I'ma street nigga, this all I know. I can't walk away. The streets owe me millions and I'ma get every dollar." I tried a soft approach 'cause I wasn't trying to lose my bitch.

"And what about your other bitches, and us getting a house together?"

"I'll try harder." I lied.

"Put it on your brothers grave." She demanded.

I wanted to lie hella bad but I couldn't disrespect my brotha's name like that and she knew it.

"I don't know why you can't just be happy with what I just promised you."

"Well, how about I start fuckin' my baby daddy and tell you to just be happy." She shot back.

"Or how about I just kill both of y'all then y'all can be happy in the ground together." She had me hot as a muthafucka now.

"See, it don't feel good, huh?"

My phone started going off right when I was really about to check her ass. I saw it was O-Dawg calling and my mood changed from irritation to optimism. I needed the plug like my life depended on it.

"O-Dawg, what's the triv, gang?" I asked with my hopes up high.

Naughty sucked her teeth, rolled her eyes then walked away with an attitude. I wasn't worried about it though 'cause I knew money and diamonds made bitches act right.

"What's brackin' lil' nigga? It took a lil' extra time but the Mob boss came through for you like I said I would. I got you in the door," he said.

I jumped up, pumping my fist in excitement. I wanted to scream but I knew that wasn't the gangsta so I kept it in. Me and Naughty's eyes locked from across the room and she didn't look happy for me.

"A'ight cool, a nigga really need this. I appreciate this shit, real talk. On gang, I ain't gon' let you down my nigga." I spoke from the heart while trying to keep my composure.

"Don't fuck this up, I'm telling you, Blood. Ain't no running off on the plug like those rap niggas be lyin' about. I put my name on this for you but I can't save you if you fuck it up." He warned.

"I hear you, gang." I assured him. "Who is it, some cartel nigga in Mexico or somethin'?"

"Naw, it's my big brotha. His name is Jaxx and he be on some other shit, you'll see. Just wait on his call. It's coming. I gotta go, Blood. It's count time."

He hung up before I could ask him all the shit I needed to know. *Fuck it.* I sat down with thoughts of being a millionaire cocaine kingpin. My whole life I hit lashes just trying to survive. But now I didn't wanna just survive, I wanted to live. I played the sidelines, watching bitch niggas get fat while we starved and robbed to eat. But now it was our turn and niggas were about to be sick. I planned on taking every muthafuckin' dollar and leaving not a penny for the opposition. And if your weren't Murdagang, then you were an opp!

I ended family day early so I could link up with the gang and put everything in motion. Naughty had an attitude the whole ride home but I didn't give a fuck. I put on Nipsey Hussle while I fantizied about the Bentley I wanted. I didn't even have a brick in my hand yet and the money was already changing me. Just the thought of millions had me not caring about my bitch or her feelings. *She better figure it out.*

Marcellus Allen

Chapter 21
Juice

It took two days for me to get the call from the plug but it was the happiest and shortest convo of my life. "This Jaxx, come to Ockly Green right now and come alone." He demanded then hung up. I rolled out the bed, threw on some clothes, grabbed my pistol then walked out without saying anything to Brittney. We'd been on rocky terms the past few days 'cause my daughter snitched on me about Bullweinkos. Brittney was mad as a muthafucka that I took Naughty and her son instead of her. So to get me back, she went on a date with one of her lesbian bitches and stayed out all night. Shit, the only thing I was mad about was she didn't bring her back to the spot with her.

I didn't pay that petty shit no mind, though. All my time and energy went to masterminding the empire I planned on building. I kept my phone glued to me every second of the hour while I waited on the call. I even got too anxious and called O-Dawg back only to find out that his phone had been disconnected! That's when the thoughts of betrayal and vengeance started running rampant through my mind. I had to force the murderous thoughts from my mind. I had to keep faith in my niggas character. So I stayed home and watched gangsta movies until I got the call.

I don't remember how long it took for me to get to the middle school but I was driving like a mad man to get there. I couldn't afford for the plug to get impatient and leave. My anxiety was that bad. When I pulled up to the front of the school, it was a few cars parked along the street. None of them stood out to me though so I circled the school looking for something foreign. My heart became discouraged after I completed my circle and saw no signs of him. He'd called private so I couldn't hit him back.

"Fuck!" I yelled as I punched the steering wheel. *They played me.* I finally came to the conclusion. My heart ached knowing I'd been betrayed by a nigga I looked up to.

I saw taillights being flashed from a black Monte Carlo parked a few feet in front of me. I drove past it the first time and he didn't flag me down. My hopes resurfaced as I pulled up next to it real slow. *Please be him.* I said to the game gods. I gripped my heat though just in case it was an enemy hoping to catch on easy body. I was anxious and desperate but not enough to just give my life away. Naw, when a nigga knocked the soul out of my body he was gon' have to work hard for it. I meant that shit from the core of my heart. I was going out trying to murder something!

My heart skipped a beat as I watched the tints roll down. I didn't know if I should shoot or keep waiting but my survival skills were getting ready to kick in. I saw a dark skinned dread head nigga come into view. He didn't have gangsta dreads like me and my niggas had, he had real dreadlocks like the Jamaicans did. *Who the fuck is this fake rasta muthafucka?*

"Leave yo phone in the car." He paused to smirk at me. "But you can bring ya pistol." Then, he rolled the window back up.

I hesitated for a second then parked the whip. I confirmed his voice as the one that called me earlier. *Leave my phone?* I already didn't like the nigga. He struck me as the real arrogant type of nigga that I killed for thrills. *Muthafucka in an old school and got the nerve to be cocky?* I thought as I parked my whip, then hopped out. I wasn't feeling leaving my phone at all. It made me feel like he wanted me vunerable or something.

"Call me Jaxx." He stuck his hand out while he stared me right in the eyes. It felt like he could read my soul. Like he knew all my secrets from just staring through me.

I was 100-percent gangsta so I didn't dare to turn my head or blink an eye. I stared right back through his trying to get a read on him. His eyes were pitch black and I knew what that meant. He'd took a few souls from the earth. He was one of them niggas that had dark secrets from the mid 90's and would never talk about them.

"They call me Juice." I gripped his hand.

"Lil' Juice, I knew yo brother a lil' bit. He was a good lil' nigga, killed before his time." He said then pulled off.

I was shocked that the plug knew who my big brotha was. I loved to run across niggas that knew him so I could hear new stories. I wanted to question him but didn't wanna seem like a scared lil' boy that missed his brotha. Murder was normal in the jungle so I needed to act like it.

"Yeah he was, but let's get down to business if you don't mind." I was ready to talk numbers.

"Never talk on the phone or in a car, that's what brought the Mafia down." He dismissed me with a wave of his hand.

That's when I really decided I didn't like the nigga. His paranoid ass watched too many movies or something. I felt like if the feds had your car bugged than you were going down anyways. But every nigga that sold bags of weed swore that the feds were on them. I guess it made unimportant niggas feel important. So I just sat back in silence and enjoyed the ride. *He lucky he O-Dawg brotha or I'd rob his bitch ass, then crush him.* An evil smirk appeared on my face.

The ride was short lived though. We pulled up to a house off the corner of 8th and Bryant in less than ten minutes. I didn't know why he felt the need to drive me that short of a distance. But I kept my mouth shut as we made our way inside the spot. We passed a few old schools on the walk but no Benzes or Bentleys. I figured his business must've been suffering since O-Dawg went to jail. I thought he sold all his foreign cars to get his bag back up. *I'ma take this shit to another level.*

"My lil' brotha trusts you. He vouches for you." He sat down, then placed a big ass Desert Eagle on the table next to a bowl of weed.

"That's my nigga, it ain't nothin' I wouldn't do for him, on gang." I vowed from the heart.

He nodded then started twisting up a Backwood.

"After all the shit he's been through, all the betrayal he's suffered from, he still trusts you. I knew Burnside since he was ten years old." He paused to light the smoke then inhaled really deep." He killed my favorite lil' cousin over his foul ass cousin then took my lil' brother to war behind it. I raised all them niggas, so forgive me when I say I don't trust you." He hit the weed while staring me down to read my reaction.

"It's impossible for us to trust each other when we don't know shit about each other. Over time, we'll learn to have trust, but for now, we'll both just trust O-Dawg."

He handed me the weed while still trying to read me. "I know some shit about you, and I have some concerns, too."

"And what's that?"

"I know what you did for my brother, and that's the only reason your sitting in my house. I respect your get-down." We locked eyes and nodded. One killa with dark secrets to another. "But my concerns are the same ones that brought lil' bro down."

"You think my niggas are rats?" I spat feeling a lil' disrespected.

"Only time will answer that, but no. Having too many enemies is what brought him down. When Burnside flipped, a lotta niggas went against lil' bro. His enemies he knew about and a shit load he didn't even know he had. And that's not even counting all the new cliques that were poppin' up. I know about all the funk you have right now and some you don't even know about. Trust me, it's too much." *This nigga a bitch, scared and shit.* I shrugged with an attitude. I already knew he was gon' use that as an excuse not to fuck with me.

"So, what you want me to do, make peace with all of them?" Just the thought of it disgusted me.

"There's no such thing in this cold game. I learned that the hard way." His eyes got darker and smaller. He was reminiscing on his dark past. "There's only enemies and niggas that are too scared to be an enemy. You can't let your enemies get up their weight or their numbers."

"So, what you want me to do then?" His wordplay had me confused.

"C'mon, I'll show you." He got up and headed out of the front room.

I shrugged then followed him down the hallway. I didn't exactly know what to expect but I kept thinking he had some nigga tied up in a room. He looked like the type that would keep somebody tied up for a few weeks.

"Aye yo, why you make me leave my phone in the car?" I asked out of nowhere.

"Cellular towers, if they ever decide to ping you, I don't want you to lead them here. I got a phone for you though that you'll only use to call me and lil' bro. I made him change his number too." He stopped at a door inside the kitchen that I knew lead to the basement.

He stared through me once more for any flaws that he might've missed earlier. But all he saw was a cold killa trapped inside a fly nigga's body. I had no flaws. I knew what the fuck I'd signed up for.

We headed down the flight of stairs then stepped into the flyest basement I'd ever seen. The carpet was plush, all the furniture easily costed a hundred bands, the TV looked like a movie theater and there was two pool tables. He lead me over to one of them that was covered with guns galore. I picked one up that had a drum on it.

"That's the Draco right there, I got three of them, " he said like I didn't know.

Every rapper in the world stayed talking about them. I'd saw a thousand pictures of it but never went and got one for some reason. But as I gripped that pretty muthafucka, I instantly fell in love. I knew she was the one for me. And the best thing was that she could fit down my pants. *Niggas in trouble now.*

"How much you want for this one?" I asked ready to pay whatever.

He shook his head slowly like I still didn't get it. "All these heats are for you and your niggas to handle y'all business. You asked what I wanted you to do about it? Kill all your enemies and leave no competition left. Come step in my office." He went and sat on the couch.

I couldn't believe the words I'd just heard. I'd always been under the impression that the connect wanted peace and to get money under the radar. But I guess the Mexican cartels had fucked that way of thinking all the way up. I smiled as I stared at all the handguns and assault rifles on the table. I wondered if he knew he was supplying the illest niggas in the town. *Yeah I fucks with this nigga.*

Marcellus Allen

Chapter 22
Juice

"So let me get this shit right, Blood," Gunna stood up from the couch and started pacing the living room. I'd been giving them the run-down for the past hour straight from the plug's mouth. It took over five hours for me and Jaxx to come up with a blueprint so I was way tired of the talking part. "He want us to start wiping all these bitch niggas out and gave us all these heats to do it?" Gunna asked.

"Yeah, he don't want nothing or nobody getting in our way of stackin' this paper. He don't care how we do it, but we need to have control of the town. So either niggas are gon' buy from us or we gon' have their mommaz bury 'em, period. Either we going all in or we leave it alone." I confirmed what I'd already said.

"Sound gucci to me." Mask spoke up.

"I'm wit it," Added Omar.

"Shit, we gon' kill most of them pussies anyways, might as well do it for a cause," TJ spoke his peace.

Flash picked up the Mac-90. "This shit seem a lil' too good to be true. How long he say 'till we get our dope?" He questioned always having to be the negative one. He was my nigga but he stayed rubbing me the wrong way.

"Whenever he get back from his spot in Miami. It should be like a week or two, enough time to start laying down the demo. If you ain't wit' it, I can just pay you for the work you already put in." I wanted to call his bluff.

"Nigga, you sound dumb as a muthafucka," He screwed his face up as he mean-mugged me. "That connect is just as much ours as it is yours. And I really ain't feeling how you're gonna be charging us an extra two thousand a brick either." He spat.

He'd been a complainer our whole lives so I didn't take his words to heart. If he'd been a new nigga than I would've knocked his brains out of his head with the .40 on my hip. I was tired of talking though so I went straight for the jugular.

"I could've kept the prices from you but I didn't. And since it's yo connect too then pull out yo phone and call him," After seconds of silence, I decided to lighten up the mood. "Now stop complaining like a bitch and start thinking about all the bitches were about to fuck and the money were about to spend." I laughed then shook his hand.

"A'ight, so who gon' get it first? And when we ridin'?" He finally gave in.

"Who y'all wanna hit first?" I asked satisfied we were all on the same page for the moment.

"Goonies." Gunna and Mask spoke at the same time. I shrugged. "Let's suit up then." I didn't care who got it first 'cause they were all already dead to me. I just wanted to hurry up and split a nigga with a Draco. We'd been laying low for a lil' minute 'cause of all of the heat we were getting. Not seeing our faces had hella niggas feeling real Braveheart on the internet but we were about to remind niggas where MurdaGang was still the illest.

An hour later we were riding in a stolen sprinter just crossing Interstate and Lombard, the streets that divided the North from North-East. We had less than ten minutes until we pulled up in the Ville.

"Yo, y'all been seeing all that peaceful shit them six-oh niggas been preaching?" Gunna broke the silence from behind the wheel.

"Yeah, that shit started in L.A and now niggas think that shit gon' work down here. Don't get me wrong, I fuckz with Nipsey but I ain't showing none of my enemies love. The first enemy I catch talkin' that black lives matter shit, I'm pushin' their shit back, on gang." Mask spoke from the heart.

I didn't feel that shit either. All the black activists in the world couldn't talk me out of killin' Freeze when he came home. They was gon' have to save that shit for the next generation. The streets had already stained my soul.

"What y'all think of those Murk unit niggas?" I changed the topic to something that concerned us.

"They aint shit, why?" Omar asked

"I'm debating on which niggas to kill and who to supply." I replied.

168

"We can work wit' them, but what about them Gas Team niggas?" Gunna said with a smirk on his face. He knew what he was doing.

"Fuck them niggas and you know damn well I ain't fuckin' wit' Jamar. If he keep speaking on me to Naughty, I'ma fuck around and crush 'em." I spat. I could feel my anger rising.

"They getting money though. We might need them nigga's business. And I know you're not letting your emotions over a bitch cloud your judgement. You wanna be El Chapo, right?" Flash added his two cents.

"Chapo is a fuckin' rat, never compare my gangsta to his." I shot back with more force than I wanted to. *I'ma just kill Jamar lowkey if need be.*

"He right, brody." Mask told me.

"Gunna, you need to be worried about them HitSquad niggas 'cause they damn sho ain't getting a pass. Either they cop from us or they die, even Breeze." I said hitting him where it hurt.

We pulled into the Ville before he could reply. We all knew it was time to do or die and kill the small talk. One slip up and we'd be living in a casket six feet in the fucking ground.

"We hoppin' out hitting whoever or we lookin' for certain niggas?" Gunna asked.

Our faces were glued to the windows looking for any nigga with dreads or sagging pants. The sun had just started going down so we knew we were gonna catch a few niggas slippin'. The Ville was known to be poppin' in the daytime with all the bitches and kids outside but when the sun went down it got really treacherous.

"Let's just ride around 'till somethin' falls in our lap." I responded.

It didn't take long for something to fall either. In less than five minutes, we found some prey to pounce on. It wasn't one of their big three but he was definitely valuable.

"Yeah, that's Jody bitch ass right there. Let's make his car his memorial sight." Mask spat.

We parked right across the street from him and he didn't even know it. He sat there in his Benz talking on the phone like he ran the city or something. But his arrogant ways was about to cost him a tab that he couldn't pay out of. It was war time and he was out in the open like he couldn't be touched. Or he didn't think niggas had the heart to come in the Ville at night. The way he looked at the van then brushed it off let me know that war was the last thing on his mind. He probably chopped it up to a soccer mom coming home.

"We gon' fill his tough ass up soon as he step out. I wanna see what this Draco do to niggas up close. Plus, I still owe these pussies a few closed caskets from spillin' a few drops of my blood." I pressed the button.

"That's what it is then." Gunna killed the engine.

Soon as the words left his mouth, the apartment door that Jody was parked in front of opened up. A short nigga walked out then started waving him in with an attitude like he'd been waiting on him.

"Who the fuck is that?" Omar asked what we were all thinking.

"I've seen his bitch ass a few times in some pictures with them niggas." Flash spoke up.

"Oh yeah? He about to get it too, then." Gunna signed his death warrant.

I watched the enemies in silence debating how I wanted to move on them. They were gonna die, but the question was how?

I stared at the unknown niggas waistline and couldn't see a bulge. It would've been easiest to slump both them pussies right then but my Jack nigga instincts kicked.

"We gon' run in the spot and take whatever those suckaz got in there, then we gon' crush 'em." I spat with murderous thoughts on my mind.

The nigga walked back inside leaving the door halfway opened. Jody was sitting halfway out the car still on his phone with a duffle bag on his lap. He really was feeling himself.

"Me, Omar and Mask gon' snatch this pussy up while y'all rush the spot. Be on point 'cause their might be some more suckaz in there. This look like their money or dope spot." I instructed.

"Well, now it's gon' be their funeral spot." Gunna vowed.

I slid the door open, then hopped out into the cold April night.

By the time Jody realized this wasn't no regular soccer van, we were already on his ass. I had the Draco pointed right at his face ready to force his mama to give him a closed casket if he tried some John Wick shit. But the fear that spread from his heart to his eyes let me know he wasn't ready to die. None of us had on Masks either so he already knew what time it was.

"Get the fuck off the phone pussy." Mask growled.

We took the phone, the bag and his pistol while the homies ran in the spot.

"How many niggas in there?" I asked.

"Man, fuck y'all niggas I ain't telling y'all shit." He decided to play tough.

"If you was really that goon brody, you would've went out in a blaze of glory instead of with your hands up like a bitch." I checked him.

"Fuck y'all niggas."

"C'mon, let's take him inside to meet up with his buddies." I put the heat to his back while forcing him to walk.

When we got inside, TJ and Flash had two niggas laying on their stomachs in the front room. I saw two pistols on the table that the enemies must have been too scared to reach for.

"Go lay yo bitch ass down next to yo homies." I told Jody.

At the sound of my voice, the two men on the floor looked up right at me. One of them was the stupid nigga that left the door open and the other was one of the main suckaz that I'd been looking for. When our eyes locked, they no longer held the fire they once did. He put his head down hoping I didn't realize who he was. Gunna came rushing down the stairs before I could toy with him. He had a backpack in his hands and a wicked smile on his face.

"I got the money, Blood," He said then looked at the bag on Omar's shoulder. "What's in there?"

"More money." Omar replied.

"Yo, that's the pussy that grazed me." I growled.

"Where!" The smile disappeared from Gunna's face.

"Stand up, Wuan, before I shoot you in the back like the coward you are." I aimed at his back.

All the eyes went on him as he struggled to his feet. He looked like a scared lil' boy instead of the killa he portrayed to be. To his credit, he managed to put a scowl on his face while muggin' me up and down.

"What the fuck you want nigga?"

"I see those last bullets I put in you didn't teach you nothin' huh? You should've took yo purple heart and moved to Atlanta or somethin', I'm disappointed in you like a real nigga. I bet that's yo pistol on the table too."

"You better kill me nigga 'cause if you don't I'm not gon' miss next time." Now his nuts were hanging.

"I believe you."

Yoppa! Yoppa! Yoppa! Yoppa! Yoppa! The Draco made him believe he could fly as he was lifted off his feet and flew to the wall. By the time he slid down to the floor, he no longer looked like the nigga he once was. His face was gone and his chest area was wide open. His blood was splattered everywhere from the walls to the ceiling. His peoples were probably just gon' cremate him.

"That's a bad muthafucka!" Gunna got hella excited.

"Which one of y'all next?" I waved it at the two bitch niggas on the ground.

"Don't shoot!"

"C'mon fam! Don't kill us!" They screamed like pussies.

"And I thought y'all was supposed to be goonz? I know y'all weak ass dead homies are turning in their graves. Tell them niggas I said fuck 'em. "I gave my hittaz the nod and then watched the fireworks.

Boom! Boom! Boom! Boc! Boc! Blocka! Blocka! They all busted their guns leaving both bodies riddled with all kinds of different bullets. There was literally smoke coming out of the bodies.

I sucked my teeth. "They died like bitches." I shook my head then walked out leaving the play gangstaz on the floor for the coroner. We were halfway across the street when we spotted two niggas rushing toward us with their smacks out. *That's what I'm talkin' about!*

"Who y'all niggas!" One of them yelled.

"The muthafuckin' predator!" I answered then did what I did best.

Yoppa! Yoppa! Yoppa! Yoppa! Blocka! Blocka! Boc! Boc! We were in a full fledge shoot-out now and I wouldn't have wanted it any other way. It had been weeks since I'd felt the rush. The hunt was on. But after they saw all the flames spittin' out of six different barrels they decided to make a smart business decision. They hauled ass. After bustin' a few shots while walking backwards, they vanished behind some town homes.

"Bitch ass niggas!' Gunna yelled after them. We hopped in the van then peeled off with the door still open just in case those suckaz tried to ambush us. I let off a few shots in the air as we sped through the blocks to let everybody know shit was real with the gang.

After five minutes of silence and letting our adrenaline die down while we escaped, I got an idea. *I still got his phone.* I started scrolling through Jody's phone until I found Rico's name. I smirked while I pressed the call button and put it on speaker.

"What it is, goon?" Rico answered.

"That nigga ain't no goon. He screamed like a bitch when real goons shot 'em." I told the truth.

"What? Who the fuck is this playin' on my phone? You must wanna die."

"This MurdaGang Juice and we ain't doing no dyin' pussy."

"Fuck Goonies, nigga!" Gunna yelled.

Then, everybody yelled the same thing along with their names. We were still riding the high from our fresh kills.

Rico sucked his teeth. "Let me guess, y'all thieving ass niggas stole the homie phone. That's all y'all known for anyway. Bum ass niggas." He started laughing then we heard some other niggas laugh too.

That shit had me hot! But I knew how to silence a crowd. "That's not what ya man's lil' Shawn would say if he could speak from the grave. And speaking of stealing, we took that bag of money from Jody right before we killed his bitch ass. Then, we killed Wuan next, did him really bad too," I shook my head like he could see me.

"His mama gon' be sick. Then, we smoked the other bitch nigga, then we stole some more money. We up four bodies pussy!" I spat.

It got quiet as a mouse after that. I could feel the heat coming through the phone. He knew I spit the truth.

"On everything I love, I'ma kill y'all mamas and y'all baby mamas then I'ma kill y'all." He whispered in hate.

"You must don't love nothin'." I hung up. I was done talking to his bitch ass. The side with the bodies didn't need to say much.

"I can't wait to catch them niggas Blood 'cause their lil' homies made it too easy. I at least want a fight." Gunna said.

While they were laughing, I was busy scrolling through his contacts. When I saw his mama number, I got an evil idea. *He wanna bring mamas into it?*

"Why are you calling me this late, Joseph?" His mother answered.

"This ain't Joseph, I'm calling you to tell you that he's dead." I said.

"What! Is this a joke? This is not not funny!" She yelled. Her pain echoed through the van.

"I'm not joking, your son is dead in the Columbia Villa right now."

She broke down crying. "Who is this? Why would somebody kill my baby! Are you one of his friends?" She asked through tears.

Everybody looked at me hoping I didn't say the gang.

"Naw, I ain't his friend." I paused for a second. "I'm the nigga that killed him. You can thank Rico, Flocko and Ace for that." I hung up then tossed the phone out the window.

"Them niggas are about to be mad as a muthafucka!" Flash said then started cracking up.

"Fuck them suckas. He shouldn't have brought mamas into it. Plus, the streets ain't show my mama no muthafuckin' sympathy. They took my brotha right in front of her." I said with venom.

"Muthafuckin' right." Omar spoke up.

My anger was rising to the max just thinking about my mama's face while my brotha's brains was splattered all over the window.

"Man fuck all that gang, put that nigga Dark Lo on. I wanna

hear some gangsta shit." I demanded then leaned back with the Draco on my lap. *Ain't no emotions in this shit.*

Marcellus Allen

Chapter 23
Juice

The next morning we were sitting outside of Faith's house hoping to catch Pistol Pete slippin'. I was hoping he thought it would be safe since most niggas would laid low after a triple homicide. Our names were hot as fish grease, but the time I made it home. But we didn't give a fuck 'cause we knew it wasn't no evidence to connect us. We had a lot of shit to get done before the plug came back home. And hiding in the house wasn't gon' help us accomplish shit. If niggas were looking for us, we planned on making it really easy for them.

It was only three of us but we were packing enough shells to get any nigga up off us. I swapped the dirty Draco out for a clean one and I was dyin' to use it.

"Y'all wanna just go inside?" I asked Gunna and Omar. I was tired of wasting time just waiting there. I had an idea.

"Kick down the door?" Gunna asked.

"Naw we gon' knock on it." I answered then hopped out the Lexus.

I knew she wasn't gon' be happy to see us but oh well. She was sleeping with the enemy and should be honored that we hadn't taken her life yet. That's how I felt. I knocked on the door and pressed the bell way too many times. We all had our heat out just in case shit got real.

"Who the hell is it?" Faith yelled.

"It's Juice, let me in."

"Juice? What the fuck you doing here?" She opened the door with an attitude. Her eyes damn near popped out of their sockets when she saw the guns we had with us. She had on a sexy ass red robe that made me think she had a nigga in there.

"I gotta holla at you about somethin', but first do you got some nigga in there?"

"Not that it's your business but no." She rolled her eyes.

We brushed right past her walking in like we owned that muthafucka. I told her to sit on the couch while the homies double checked her story. She sat there staring daggers at me until they returned.

"A'ight, let me talk to her one on one really quick." I told them. They nodded then went back to the car.

"You did all this for what? This shit was so unnecessary." She said a lil' too calm for me.

Most bitches would've been crying and screaming while asking a hundred questions. But she was calm. She knew exactly why I was there.

"You know why I'm here Faith, so let's get down to business. Where that bitch nigga at?" I laid the Draco on the table then sat down.

"I don't know, Davontae." She lied.

I massaged my temples trying to control my anger.

"Yeah, you do and I'm starting to get really mad. Your protecting a pussy that got money on my head. I really don't wanna kill you."

"I don't have nothing to do with that. You're the one that stole his money or whatever, not me."

"So that's the lie he told you, huh? A'ight, fuck it, you can die with yo' nigga then." I growled then jumped up with the barrel touching her head.

She screamed then started pleading. "Wait! Don't shoot me, Juice!"

"Wait for what? You ready to die right? You think niggas is out here playin'! Me and my niggas are out here killin' every day just to stay alive bitch. While you out there fuckin' dope boyz for money were hunting to stay alive. Now ask yourself is that sucka worth dyin' for 'cause he don't give a fuck about you! You ready to die! Huh?" I screamed with my finger itching to pull the trigga.

All she could do was shake her head while she cried her soul out. Even though she stayed hating on me, I had no desire to take her life. But I had two daughters that expected for me to walk through their bedroom doors on the regular. So anybody that tried to prevent that from happening had to get it. Them, their family and their side bitches. *I got an idea.*

"Yo where your phone at?" I asked.

She pulled it from her pocket and tried to hand it over.

"Call that nigga, I'ma show you how much he love you." I took the gun from her head. "Put it on speaker and tell him you're in trouble." I instructed.

She nodded then did what I said.

"Hello?" He answered on the third ring.

Just hearing his voice made me wanna kill something.

"Baby? He got me!" She cried. *He? They been talking about me.*

"What?" He replied.

I snatched the phone. "You thought you could put a bag on me and I wasn't gon' come see about you? Now I'ma hurt them pockets. We want 50,000 thousand or I'ma crush this bitch right now and let you listen to her take her last breath." I threatened.

He chuckled. "It's cheaper for you to keep her." He spat like it was nothing.

Her hands shot to her mouth in shock as the tears rolled down her face.

"Oh, you think I'm playing, nigga?"

"Naw, I know you're serious. She got some good pussy but fuck her dumb ass. And when I catch you, I'ma bury you next to your bitch ass brother." He laughed then hung up.

"You ready to help me now or you still wanna play ride or die chick? 'Cause now it's personal." He had disrespected my brotha and for that he moved to the top of my kill list.

"What do you wanna know?" She wiped away her last tear with malice in her voice.

Forty-five minutes later, we were pulling up on Haight and Shaver St., where a park was located at. The area was controlled by the Denver Lane niggas and was one of the goldmines for selling dope. It was also the hood I'd grown up in.

"Look at these niggas standing out here." Omar commented on the two niggas standing on the corner sticking out.

"They ain't trying to let their hood go."

The unthanks were the last niggas refusing to lose their turf to gentrification but their time was coming, it was inevitable. Most of them were already relocated to the numbers but would make the thirty minute drive just to post up.

"Shit, hopefully these niggas get with the program 'cause we don't need to be beefin' with them too. I mean anybody can get it but we do need niggas to buy or dope." Gunna added.

"We're about to find out." I hopped out ready to get down to business. I really wasn't worried about it too much 'cause I knew how to handle the cats I grew up with. My mind was still on me and Faith's conversation and how bad I wanted to spill his blood.

"What's brackin' wit' y'all?" Ghost walked up on us with some young nigga I'd never met.

"What's good with it?" I dapped him up followed by Gunna and Omar.

"Holding it down, you already know, Blood. Stix and Notchie in there waiting for you."

We shook him up again then walked in the house. They both were posted on the couch twisting up a wood, looking like they ain't have shit else to do. They instantly got sparked when we walked in.

"What's good with my young killaz!" Notchie hopped up being hella dramatic.

"What's poppin' with y'all?" We shook them up then sat down on the couch.

"A'ight, tell us about this business deal you was bragging about on the phone." Stix being the real hustla, got straight down to business.

I nodded in agreement then started laying out our blueprint. They listened for ten minutes without saying a word while I explained how we could all profit from my proposition. Notchie kept nodding his head while Stix just stared through me. It was hard to get a read on him but I knew the money talked and the bullshit walked a thousand miles.

"So, you're about to be the new plug in the town, huh? That's a big leap." Stix was the first one to speak.

"I got big dreams and even bigger guns to go with 'em." I shot back.

"We'll see." He waved his hand not sounding impressed at all. "So, we buy from you at a cheaper price than we pay Ray-Ray and D-Roc, and the work is gon' be better? You got some product with you?"

"Naw, it's at the spot." I lied.

"Bring some to me and we can work it out from there."

I was hella irritated but had to keep my frustration in check. I could relate to his concerns though.

"Y'all know y'all gon' have to kill them Gas Team niggas, right?" Notchie asked with a smile on his face.

"They're already dead in our book." Gunna spoke up.

"Good ' cause I don't like bloods and crips teaming up anyways. I don't know what kinda shit that is or where the fuck they do that at." The disgust was heard clearly in his voice.

When Ray-Ray, who was a blood and his Crip cousin D-Roc started the Gas Team about two years ago nobody had took them seriously or thought it would work. But them niggas had recently took off and was getting money while piling up bodies.

"We gon' handle it."

"If you was from the hood your supposed to be from, this shit could have been much easier." Stix spoke his mind.

Here we go with this shit. "I'm always goin' rep the hood but you know I'm not with that blood and crip shit. Plus you know I'm not good with following rules." I laughed a lil' bit to ease the let-down.

We chopped it up another couple of minutes then we walked out with one more box checked on our long list. All I needed was for Jaxx to come back and drop those bricks on me so we could really start showing the streets what time it was.

"You think we should hit up those Murk unit niggas now or later?" Omar asked after we pulled out of the neighborhood.

It was something on our check list that we had to do but I felt like it was bad timing. The Murk unit was a click full of crips ran by Teflon and Shotta that stayed beefing with niggas throughout the town.

Their top niggas got money, but the twenty niggas under them didn't care about nothing except killing. *They deep as a muthafucka.*

"Naw, we gon' hold off on them right now. We don't know how their gonna respond and once a threat has been laid down we gotta back it up. We gonna have a sitdown with 'em after we wipe a few of these other suckas out the box." I answered.

"Don't matter to me, we can get 'em now or get 'em later. Fuck those niggas." Gunna spoke his usual truth.

"We need to step our numbers up too. A lotta them other niggas are way deeper than us."

"So what, I'd rather ten lions than a hundred sheep."

"You right, but I'd rather have a hundred lions than just ten." I shot back.

"So, you wanna bring niggas into our circle now?" Omar jumped in. He was the most clanish out of the whole circle.

"Not our Inner circle but we do needa start adding niggas to the Squad. Were gonna need more shooters on our side thats loyal to us."

"What you got in mind?" Gunna asked.

"How y'all feel about JoJo and his drama gang niggas?"

Chapter 24
Juice

It took a week for Jaxx to hit my line but when he did I jetted out of the house feeling like all of my hard work was finally paying off. The past week had been filled with nothing but drama and shoot outs all in the name of the almighty dollar. The crazy thing was outside of the money we took from them soft ass Goonie niggas we hadn't made a dolla. Every shell we dropped and every move that was made was done for the future. The hope for the future.

After Jody's snitchin' ass mama got on the news and told the whole city how the killa called n had led her phone the streets went crazy. Of course, the haters were all over Facebook dry snitchin' like a muthafucka. We like they actually saw the shit. We weren't trippin' off of it though, that's how the game was played now days. The good thing was that stunt really pumped fear into the underworld. They got to witness firsthand how ruthless and cold hearted we could be. It also forced Rico, Flocko and Ace to step their gangsta up. They'd caught Mask coming out of the barber shop and tried to end his life to no avail. They were driving all around Portland in a stolen blue Nissan looking for revenge. They were hopping out on hella niggas asking about our whereabouts. We weren't worried though.

Then to make matters worse all the bitches in my life had to be on their periods at the same damn time. Naughty called my phone livid about the way we popped up at Faith's house screaming and cussing. I had to check her dumb ass then everything went downhill from there.

I ended up taking her her whip back and we agreed to call it quits. But we've done that multiple times so I didn't take it serious at all. Latoya was still on her trip over her sucka baby dad and Brittney kept forcing that relationship shit. But I forced all of that to the back of my mind as I parked the rented Malibu in the apartment complex Jaxx told me to come to.

"What's good with it?" I gave Jaxx a G-hug as I walked in.

"It's hood on my end, everything good with y'all?" He replied then lead me through the hallway.

The apartment was empty of all signs of life except for a table and a couch. But on the table sat multiple stacks of cocaine that made my heart skip a beat. It was at that moment that I really knew I'd made it from a half not nigga to a half got nigga. I knew my destiny was in my hands. With the heart of a warrior in my chest and a .45 on my hip, I was ready to run the city.

"We've been building the foundation for the work and pumping fear in our enemies. They know their time on earth is almost up. I just need the work." I told him

He nodded then tossed me a brick. "I see you brough a rental like I told you."

"Yeah, I copped it right after I left yo spot and had it waiting. And I left my other phone at the house too."

"A'ight, make sure you do it like that every time. Never drive the same whip over here twice and don't ever tell a soul about this place. For now on this gon' be your pickup location. I'ma show you where the safe at and get you a key too."

"Yeah, this spot seem lowkey too. I'ma fuck around and cop a spot out here. I ain't never really played Beaverton or Aloha like that."

"It's good to switch yo spots up, especially to another city. But let's get down to business. I got fifteen bricks for you right now, can you handle it?"

I did the numbers in my head and came up a lil' short but I couldn't tell him that. I knew if I did than he would lose confidence in my hustle. I was gone have to take them and lay my hustle game down hard.

"Yeah we can move them," I picked up another brick and nodded. "How fast you need me to move 'em?"

"Fast as you can and there's plenty more that needs to be moved. That's why I told you killin' your enemies is a win-win. You stay alive and get to take their money. This is what you asked for right? You're in the big leagues now, Ain't no more petty shit."

I knew he was right so I forced any doubt out of my mind and heart. "I'm ready." Was all I said.

He cracked a smile. "Good, 'cause I'm expecting you to move at least thirty a month."

I felt the doubt creep back in but I would've never admitted it to him. It was do or die time, fo'real.

A few hours later, we were at Mask's bitch house out in the numbers discussing our plans. We had to slide out that way instead of Omars spot 'cause some Hoover nigga had popped somebody in the lot and gangtas was deep. I wasn't trippin' 'cause she had a big ass basement for us to post up in. I had all of the dope laid out on the table while I paced listening to all of their suggestions on how we should move forward.

"We gon' have to get those Gas Team niggas out the way sooner than later. Them suckaz taking up too much of the pie." Gunna spat.

"On gang." Flash agreed with him like always.

"TJ, what you over there thinking?" I asked the homie. He was always quiet as hell but stayed having the best ideas.

"We gon' have to knock some niggas down in order to come up. Either we gon' have to take over some hoods and start pushin' our shit or kill off the cliques that's supplying them. I say we finish the Goonies off, then set up shop." He whispered.

"Y'all wanna post up in the North?" I asked.

"All we gotta do is find some other niggas out there who don't fuck with them and put them in position." Mask added.

I thought really hard about what he was saying. I nodded once I started seeing the bigger picture.

"So, let some other niggas move in but force them to cop from us?" I questioned the group.

"Exactly." Mask answered.

"Who y'all wanna fuck with on that tip?"

"We'll figure that out later. Let's just hurry up and murder these suckaz." Gunna spat.

"A'ight bet, but in the meantime we gotta move this shit right now." I pointed at the bricks.

"Everybody take two and move that shit. I'ma save three for them Drama Gang niggas when we link up with them."

"So, we fuckin' with them?" TJ asked.

"I hollered at JoJo and it sound like they with it. It's ten of those lil' niggas, they gon' come in handy. They young and wild and JoJo look at me like I'm his big bro. We gon' meet up with them and check out their vibe." I replied.

I had plans for them lil' niggas that would benefit the team in a major way. And as long as they stayed loyal , they was gon' get rich with us and run these streets right beside us.

My phone went off. Interrupting us. I answered on speaker when I saw who it was.

"What's poppin' big bro? You on speaker with all the homies."

"What's Mobbin' with my young killahz? This the Mob Boss himself!" O-Dawg got hella excited.

"What's brackin' Blood!" Gunna threw up gang signs like he could see him.

Everybody took turns showing the homie some love then he got down to business.

"I was calling to let you know I just got my first visit with my son and a nigga really appreciate what y'all did." He told us.

"It's all love fam, you know that." I responded.

"Plus, I heard shit went good today. I'm guessing y'all sitting around right now trying to come up with some plays." He laughed a lil' bit already knowing the triv.

"Yeah, we trying to make it happen."

"I'm confident y'all gon' do that. But let me give y'all some game on a few things really quick. When real money comes into play, niggas egos gotta stay in check. I'm talkin' about with each other. The loyalty amongst y'all circle gotta be strong as iron. You can't let no nigga or bitch come in between y'all period. And there can't be no secrets either, the muthafuckaz are cancer. We let pride, a bitch and a few secrets crush our whole dynasty. My closest niggas are in the grave behind that shit, Blood."

We could feel his pain pour through the phone and sit over our heads like a black cloud. This wasn't no nigga we'd read about in the Don Diva or seen his documentary on Gangland. He was speaking about a war that we personally witnessed fuck our city up. A war I'd actually caught a few bodies in. So when he spoke, we could hear the pain and betrayal behind his words. We could visualize seeing niggas we grew up looking up to laying in a casket. The shit was real.

We all looked at each other with the same somber expressions on our faces. We knew we couldn't go out the same way they did.

"Would you do it all again if you could?" I asked the question I felt we all wanted to know.

He sighed really deep. "I would definitely play the game all over again. I'ma legand in these Portland streets and ain't nothin' more important than that. I made millions in North-East. Hell naw I wouldn't take it back, fuck naw! The only thing I would do different is how we handled Jersey Joe. I would bring the facts to Burnside first then killed Joe. That secret broke our bond."

"I feel you, big bro."

"Y'all lil' niggas need to enjoy the ride though, Blood. When everything is all said and done and your sitting in a cell, all you'll have is your name and your memories. Go hard on them haters. Cop every car, fuck every bitch and shut down every club. Y'all not Jack boyz that need to stay in the dark no more. If y'all wanna be the kings of the town, then act like it. It come with the territory. But this bitch calling my other line, I'll tap-in later."

He hung up and we sat there quiet, still soaking up all the jewels he dropped on us. I knew I had to say somethin'.

"No secrets, no jealousy and no fuckin' on each other's baby mamas or main bitches. The first nigga to betray our rules gotta die, even me. We can't go out like they did gang. If we gotta go out, then we going out together. No snitchin' or switchin' sides, Murda Gang or don't bang."

"MurdaGang or don't bang!" They all shot back at me.

The next day, I was up early on my grizzy with a bird sitting on the backseat of the Escalade.

This nigga I fucked with from the north named Capone wanted to cop a whole thang. He was a mid-level nigga that would be good for a few birds a month. I also planned on picking his brain about all of those Goonie suckaz enemies. I wanted them out of the way asap.

I hit his phone as I parked at George Park. He told me he was bending the corner at the moment. I gripped the .40 in my hoody as I looked around the scenery. Every time I went to the North, my paranoia kicked into overdrive. The shit was foreign land to me. But it was hella money out that bitch and I wanted it.

I watched a black Caprice turn the corner and park a few feet away. It was too early for anybody to be going to the park so I knew it was Capone. I looked around again and the streets were empty and silent. I hit my horn then he hit his back. I grabbed the bag ready to make the deal and get the fuck out of there. He hopped out and waved me over. *Let's hurry up and get this shit over with.*

I bounced out mad that I had to get out in the cold. When he saw I had the bag, he reached in and pulled one out.

"Why you ain't come get in? I wanted to holla at you?" I complained.

"Oh, my bad." He said and stood there like he wanted me to keep walking toward him.

I froze in my tracks, something was off. His body language was weird. The look on his face didn't match a hustla that was coppin' a brick. He seemed mad.

I noticed how close his hand was to his waist and I didn't know if he was being cautious or was gonna reach.

"You just gon' stand there or what?" I asked with my chest poked out.

He stood there confused not saying nothing. I was really starting to think he'd set me up with the feds and was getting ready to run until the back door opened up. As soon as Rico popped his head out my gangsta overrode my fear.

Boom! Boom! Boom! Boc! Boc! Boc! Bloc! Bloc! I hit Capone's hoe ass right in the chest before he could even pull his heat. He crumbled instantly to the pavement then me and Rico banged it out. Before I knew it, Ace and Flocko bounced out slangin' their irons too. The hate was written all on their faces. I waved my pistol between the three of them trying to knock somethin' down. They weren't taking cover or nothing. They just kept on walking up on some ready to die Terminator type of shit. They really wanted me dead.

"This what y'all niggas want!" I yelled while backpedaling to my truck.

"Don't run, bitch!" Rico taunted.

We exchanged shots until I got hit in my left shoulder forcing me to drop the bag in pain. "Agghh!" I screamed out then kept bustin' my heat.

We went shot for shot until I realized I was in a no-win situation. Every step I took backwards, them niggas took forward. I knew eventually they were gonna surround me and that was gone be the end of my life. I let off a few more shots then turned around to run to the truck.

I made it a few steps before I felt a bullet hit my back, forcing me to fly down to one knee. My pistol flew out of my hand then slid across the pavement out of my reach. I bounced up then sprinted across the street praying I didn't catch one to the back of my head.

I could hear the bullets whizzing past my head every step I took. It seemed like I could hear them niggas footsteps inside my head. I was expecting to drop at any moment. But I didn't. I hopped a fence landing in somebody's backyard then hopped up and kept hauling ass. For the split second I hit the ground I could see them niggas crossing the street still trying to body me. The gunshots never stopped raining down on me. It felt like lightning and thunder was trying to strike me at the same time.

My back was pounding like a muthafucka but my adrenaline was keeping me alive. I hit another fence then dove under a car that was parked in a driveway. The only sound that could be heard was police sirens. I could hear my heart pounding in my ears. I pulled my phone out and called Gunna.

"What's it is, gang?" He answered.

"I'm hit, gang." I groaned.

"Blood, stop playing."

"On Juice, I'm hit. They got me at George Park. The Goonies."

"Nigga, what! Where you at?" He screamed.

I heard voices getting closer and got scared to answer him

"Where the fuck that nigga go?"

"I don't know which way he went. I know we hit him a few times, bitch ass nigga."

I hung the phone up 'cause I could hear Gunna still yelling through it. Two pairs of feet was standing right next to the car I was under. I'd never been more scared in my life. Then I heard a car pull up and one of them started yelling.

"You see the nigga?"

"Naw! C'mon nigga, the boyz almost here!"

"Fuck, how we let his bitch ass get away." It sounded like Rico.

I held my breath until I saw their shoes sprint off and heard the car doors slam. Soon as they skirted off I rolled out then called Gunna back.

"Hello! We all on the way!" He answered yelling.

I looked up at the sky for a few seconds just enjoying the view. I never appreciated the beauty of it before. I felt the blood pouring out of my body pint by pint and knew I was bleeding to death. Just when I was giving up the fight my mind flashed to my brotha. I couldn't die before I killed Freeze, fuck that! I couldn't let Juice down like that.

"Agghh!" I growled as I pulled myself up to my feet. I wasn't dyin' on my back like no bitch ass nigga. I walked to the street so I could see where I was at. "I'm right at the corner by the old shamrock." I finally responded to Gunna.

"We pullin' up, blood! The pigs is out everywhere!"

I sat on the corner until they found me. I'd never been happier in my life to see my niggas. Gunna and Flash jumped out and helped me to the backseat. Flash got in the back with me while Gunna peeled out.

"Where you hit, blood?" Gunna asked.

"I don't know. My arm and back, I think. Capone set me up, I popped that nigga." I whispered feeling hella groggy.

"You gon' be a'ight. Niggas get shot everyday, B. You tough right?" Flash thought he was Cam'ron.

"Fuck you, nigga."

"We gon' kill all them niggas, on gang. Gunna, hurry the fuck up! This nigga bleeding like a muthafucka! Juice, who was it?"

"Rico, Ace and Flocko." I barely got out.

"Nigga, keep yo eyes open!" He started shaking me.

But I couldn't. I was tired as a muthafucka and just wanted to go to sleep. I was gon' kill them niggas but I needed my sleep first. I heard them both yelling but couldn't understand what they were saying. I really didn't care. I was tired. Then everything went black.

Marcellus Allen

Chapter 25
Naughty

I woke up to Jamar whispering into his phone. I laid there being still as I could so I could eaves drop on the conversation. I was hoping to catch him on there with a bitch so I could flip the fuck out. He spent house last night convincing me to give our family another chance. I told him I would then we made love for hours. Juice had shown me that I wasn't worth shit to him when he let me walk away without putting up a fight. Jamar was really putting in the work while Juice ran the streets and acted like I didn't mean shit.

"So, the nigga dead?" He asked sounding real excited.

"We was gon' have to kill 'em anyway, plus he was probably gon' trip about me and Naughty anyways. Fuck that nigga."

My heart jumped out of my chest. I knew he was talking about Juice. A wave of emotions hit me at one time. I shot straight up in shock. He looked at me then hurried out of the room. I grabbed my phone and turned it on. *50 missed calls? Please God, don't let him be dead!* I prayed while the tears fell down my face. I called his mother, but she didn't answer. Then, I tried Gunna, but he didn't either. Just when I was redialing his mother my brother JoJo started calling me. I hoped that he had some info for me.

"Tell me he ain't dead, JoJo!" I cried.

"Naw, he in surgery right now. We up here at the hospital right now." He told me.

I felt a wave of relief.

"Who's we?"

"All my niggas and his. We were supposed to meet today, then this shit happened." He spat.

"Meet you for what?"

"We all one movement now, sis. So, whoever popped him gotta deal with us now. Just get yo ass up here." He hung up.

One movement? They'd always been cool, but I didn't know they'd gotten that close. My lil' brother and his homies were even worse that Juice and his. I really hoped Jamar had nothing to do with it. *Fuck!* I hopped up to get dressed and Jamar was standing in the doorway staring at me.

"Where you going?"

"You know where," I answered.

"That nigga about to die."

I started getting dressed, not even responding to his fuckery. He stopped me at the door.

"You're not going to see another nigga while you're my bitch." It was a threat.

I mugged him. "That's a choice you gotta make. Let me know when I get back." Then I pushed him out the way and hopped in my car. "Please, God, don't let him die!" I screamed out.

To Be Continued…
The Streets Stained My Soul 2
Coming Soon

Submission Guideline

Submit the first three chapters of your completed manuscript to ldpsubmissions@gmail.com, subject line: Your book's title. The manuscript must be in a .doc file and sent as an attachment. Document should be in Times New Roman, double spaced and in size 12 font. Also, provide your synopsis and full contact information. If sending multiple submissions, they must each be in a separate email.

Have a story but no way to send it electronically? You can still submit to LDP/Ca$h Presents. Send in the first three chapters, written or typed, of your completed manuscript to:

LDP: Submissions Dept
Po Box 870494
Mesquite, Tx 75187

DO NOT send original manuscript. Must be a duplicate.

Provide your synopsis and a cover letter containing your full contact information.

Thanks for considering LDP and Ca$h Presents.

Coming Soon from Lock Down Publications/Ca$h Presents

BOW DOWN TO MY GANGSTA

By **Ca$h**

TORN BETWEEN TWO

By **Coffee**

THE STREETS STAINED MY SOUL **II**

By **Marcellus Allen**

BLOOD OF A BOSS **VI**

SHADOWS OF THE GAME II

By **Askari**

LOYAL TO THE GAME **IV**

By **T.J. & Jelissa**

A DOPEBOY'S PRAYER **II**

By **Eddie "Wolf" Lee**

IF LOVING YOU IS WRONG... **III**

By **Jelissa**

TRUE SAVAGE **VII**

MIDNIGHT CARTEL

DOPE BOY MAGIC II

By **Chris Green**

BLAST FOR ME **III**

DUFFLE BAG CARTEL **IV**

HEARTLESS GOON **IV**

A SAVAGE DOPEBOY II

DRUG LORDS III

By **Ghost**

A HUSTLER'S DECEIT III

KILL ZONE **II**

BAE BELONGS TO ME III

The Streets Stained My Soul

SOUL OF A MONSTER III

By **Aryanna**

THE COST OF LOYALTY **III**

By **Kweli**

THE SAVAGE LIFE III

CHAINED TO THE STREETS II

By **J-Blunt**

KING OF NEW YORK V

COKE KINGS IV

BORN HEARTLESS IV

By **T.J. Edwards**

GORILLAZ IN THE BAY V

De'Kari

THE STREETS ARE CALLING II

Duquie Wilson

KINGPIN KILLAZ IV

STREET KINGS III

PAID IN BLOOD III

CARTEL KILLAZ IV

Hood Rich

SINS OF A HUSTLA II

ASAD

TRIGGADALE III

Elijah R. Freeman

KINGZ OF THE GAME V

Playa Ray

SLAUGHTER GANG IV

RUTHLESS HEART II

By Willie Slaughter

THE HEART OF A SAVAGE II

Marcellus Allen

By Jibril Williams

FUK SHYT II

By Blakk Diamond

THE DOPEMAN'S BODYGAURD II

By Tranay Adams

TRAP GOD II

By Troublesome

YAYO II

A SHOOTER'S AMBITION II

By S. Allen

GHOST MOB

Stilloan Robinson

KINGPIN DREAMS II

By Paper Boi Rari

CREAM

By Yolanda Moore

SON OF A DOPE FIEND II

By Renta

FOREVER GANGSTA II

By Adrian Dulan

LOYALTY AIN'T PROMISED

By Keith Williams

THE PRICE YOU PAY FOR LOVE II

By Destiny Skai

THE LIFE OF A HOOD STAR

By Rashia Wilson

TOE TAGZ II

By Ah'Million

CONFESSIONS OF A GANGSTA II

By Nicholas Lock

Available Now

RESTRAINING ORDER **I & II**

By **CA$H & Coffee**

LOVE KNOWS NO BOUNDARIES **I II & III**

By **Coffee**

RAISED AS A GOON I, II, III & IV

BRED BY THE SLUMS I, II, III

BLAST FOR ME I & II

ROTTEN TO THE CORE I II III

A BRONX TALE I, II, III

DUFFEL BAG CARTEL I II III

HEARTLESS GOON

A SAVAGE DOPEBOY

HEARTLESS GOON I II III

DRUG LORDS I II

By **Ghost**

LAY IT DOWN **I & II**

LAST OF A DYING BREED

BLOOD STAINS OF A SHOTTA I & II III

By **Jamaica**

LOYAL TO THE GAME

LOYAL TO THE GAME II

LOYAL TO THE GAME III

LIFE OF SIN I, II III

By **TJ & Jelissa**

BLOODY COMMAS I & II

SKI MASK CARTEL I II & III

KING OF NEW YORK I II,III IV

Marcellus Allen

RISE TO POWER I II III

COKE KINGS I II III

BORN HEARTLESS I II III

By **T.J. Edwards**

IF LOVING HIM IS WRONG…I & II

LOVE ME EVEN WHEN IT HURTS I II III

By **Jelissa**

WHEN THE STREETS CLAP BACK I & II III

By **Jibril Williams**

A DISTINGUISHED THUG STOLE MY HEART I II & III

LOVE SHOULDN'T HURT I II III IV

RENEGADE BOYS I II III IV

By **Meesha**

A GANGSTER'S CODE I &, II III

A GANGSTER'S SYN I II III

THE SAVAGE LIFE I II

CHAINED TO THE STREETS

By J-Blunt

PUSH IT TO THE LIMIT

By **Bre' Hayes**

BLOOD OF A BOSS **I, II, III, IV, V**

SHADOWS OF THE GAME

By **Askari**

THE STREETS BLEED MURDER **I, II & III**

THE HEART OF A GANGSTA I II& III

By **Jerry Jackson**

CUM FOR ME

CUM FOR ME 2

CUM FOR ME 3

CUM FOR ME 4

The Streets Stained My Soul

CUM FOR ME 5

An **LDP Erotica Collaboration**

BRIDE OF A HUSTLA **I II & II**

THE FETTI GIRLS **I, II& III**

CORRUPTED BY A GANGSTA I, II III, IV

BLINDED BY HIS LOVE

THE PRICE YOU PAY FOR LOVE

By **Destiny Skai**

WHEN A GOOD GIRL GOES BAD

By **Adrienne**

THE COST OF LOYALTY I II

By Kweli

A GANGSTER'S REVENGE **I II III & IV**

THE BOSS MAN'S DAUGHTERS

THE BOSS MAN'S DAUGHTERS II

THE BOSSMAN'S DAUGHTERS III

THE BOSSMAN'S DAUGHTERS IV

THE BOSS MAN'S DAUGHTERS **V**

A SAVAGE LOVE **I & II**

BAE BELONGS TO ME I II

A HUSTLER'S DECEIT I, II, III

WHAT BAD BITCHES DO I, II, III

SOUL OF A MONSTER I II

KILL ZONE

By **Aryanna**

A KINGPIN'S AMBITON

A KINGPIN'S AMBITION **II**

I MURDER FOR THE DOUGH

By **Ambitious**

TRUE SAVAGE

Marcellus Allen

TRUE SAVAGE II

TRUE SAVAGE III

TRUE SAVAGE IV

TRUE SAVAGE V

TRUE SAVAGE VI

DOPE BOY MAGIC

MIDNIGHT CARTEL

By **Chris Green**

A DOPEBOY'S PRAYER

By **Eddie "Wolf" Lee**

THE KING CARTEL **I, II & III**

By **Frank Gresham**

THESE NIGGAS AIN'T LOYAL **I, II & III**

By **Nikki Tee**

GANGSTA SHYT **I II &III**

By **CATO**

THE ULTIMATE BETRAYAL

By **Phoenix**

BOSS'N UP **I , II & III**

By **Royal Nicole**

I LOVE YOU TO DEATH

By Destiny J

I RIDE FOR MY HITTA

I STILL RIDE FOR MY HITTA

By **Misty Holt**

LOVE & CHASIN' PAPER

By **Qay Crockett**

TO DIE IN VAIN

SINS OF A HUSTLA

By **ASAD**

The Streets Stained My Soul

BROOKLYN HUSTLAZ

By **Boogsy Morina**

BROOKLYN ON LOCK I & II

By **Sonovia**

GANGSTA CITY

By **Teddy Duke**

A DRUG KING AND HIS DIAMOND I & II III

A DOPEMAN'S RICHES

HER MAN, MINE'S TOO I, II

CASH MONEY HO'S

By Nicole Goosby

TRAPHOUSE KING **I II & III**

KINGPIN KILLAZ I II III

STREET KINGS I II

PAID IN BLOOD **I II**

CARTEL KILLAZ I II III

By **Hood Rich**

LIPSTICK KILLAH **I, II, III**

CRIME OF PASSION I II & III

By **Mimi**

STEADY MOBBN' **I, II, III**

THE STREETS STAINED MY SOUL

By **Marcellus Allen**

WHO SHOT YA **I, II, III**

SON OF A DOPE FIEND

Renta

GORILLAZ IN THE BAY **I II III IV**

DE'KARI

TRIGGADALE I II

Elijah R. Freeman

Marcellus Allen

GOD BLESS THE TRAPPERS I, II, III
THESE SCANDALOUS STREETS I, II, III
FEAR MY GANGSTA I, II, III
THESE STREETS DON'T LOVE NOBODY I, II
BURY ME A G I, II, III, IV, V
A GANGSTA'S EMPIRE I, II, III, IV
THE DOPEMAN'S BODYGAURD
Tranay Adams
THE STREETS ARE CALLING
Duquie Wilson
MARRIED TO A BOSS... I II III
By Destiny Skai & Chris Green
KINGZ OF THE GAME I II III IV
Playa Ray
SLAUGHTER GANG I II III
RUTHLESS HEART
By Willie Slaughter
THE HEART OF A SAVAGE
By Jibril Williams
FUK SHYT
By Blakk Diamond
DON'T F#CK WITH MY HEART I II
By Linnea
ADDICTED TO THE DRAMA I II III
By Jamila
YAYO
A SHOOTER'S AMBITION
By S. Allen
TRAP GOD
By Troublesome

FOREVER GANGSTA

By Adrian Dulan

TOE TAGZ

By Ah'Million

KINGPIN DREAMS

By Paper Boi Rari

CONFESSIONS OF A GANGSTA

By Nicholas Lock

BOOKS BY LDP'S CEO, CA$H

TRUST IN NO MAN

TRUST IN NO MAN 2

TRUST IN NO MAN 3

BONDED BY BLOOD

SHORTY GOT A THUG

THUGS CRY

THUGS CRY 2

THUGS CRY 3

TRUST NO BITCH

TRUST NO BITCH 2

TRUST NO BITCH 3

TIL MY CASKET DROPS

RESTRAINING ORDER

RESTRAINING ORDER 2

IN LOVE WITH A CONVICT

Coming Soon

BONDED BY BLOOD 2

BOW DOWN TO MY GANGSTA

The Streets Stained My Soul

www.ingramcontent.com/pod-product-compliance
Lightning Source LLC
Chambersburg PA
CBHW070503260626
47161CB00004B/1429